All Hands

Spineless Wonders
PO Box 220
STRAWBERRY HILLS
New South Wales, Australia, 2012
shortaustralianstories.com.au

First published by Spineless Wonders 2019
Text copyright © Megan McGrath 2019
Cover design by Bettina Kaiser
Typesetting by Heike Krieger | BKA+D
Published by Bronwyn Mehan. Assistant editor,
Hannah Janssen. Publishing assistants Siobhan Doig, Prashant
Prasad. Publicist, Hannah Oakshott.

Typeset in Franklin Gothic Book
Printed and bound by Ingram Spark
All Hands/Megan McGrath
ISBN 978-1-925052-40-4

Distribution in Australia and New Zealand by New South

A catalogue record for this
book is available from the
National Library of Australia

This project has been assisted by the Copyright Agency Cultural Fund.

C©PYRIGHTAGENCY
CULTURAL FUND

All Hands

Collected stories

Megan McGrath

Contents

Brother Bird

I lose sight of him on the paddle back out. The swell is thick with foam, churned by the backwash off the gnarled cliff-face. It was dangerous to bring my brother to this side of the headland, with his soft-topped board and milky bones, but it was the only place out of the wind, away from the stingers, and he wanted to check on the birds.

It's not until his board bumps my ankle that panic floods me. The set is coming and I grab his squishy rail and paddle for shore like the last girl alive.

When my brother comes out of the white-wash, he's wrought. His mouth ajar, caught in a gasp, or a cry, I can't tell. He's holding his cupped hands out in front of him.

In the shallows, I tear off my leash and let our boards wash ashore. My eyes search him for bite-marks and flesh wounds as I stagger through the breakers to reach him.

I'm hoarse from calling out when I say, 'Are you alright?'

The current tugs at our feet as I steady him.

He's lost his words, but he peels his palms apart to reveal a hatchling, still wet with membrane, once a bird, now reduced to feathers and crushed bone.

I hear them now, the children gathered by the rock. Their battle-cries caught on the southerly. And I see her, the mother curlew, with wings wide, bleating out a desperate hiss in her defence. She's backed into the dune grass, just a bird against these mongrel blow-ins with their peeling shoulders and boardshorts from Country Road.

'Here, let me,' I tell my brother. He is pink with tears as I take the baby bird from his fingers. His hands remain cupped, empty. 'Take our boards up,' I say and before he can point out I never let him touch my stick, I add, 'Hurry.'

I piece it together, watching a girl of about eight throwing rocks into the shore-break. Not rocks.

Eggs.

He's been harbouring these birds for weeks. Checking on the eggs every day. As I watch, his handmade cardboard signs flap in the wind ripping around the headland. Birds Nesting: Keep Out. I should have known his warning would be a beacon to the tourist kids.

He wanted to sit with the nest, instead I'd coaxed him into the surf, a swell too big and too full of chop for him anyway.

Now, I shield the dead chick in my hand as I run up the cove to the nest, calves burning across soft sand.

The mother bird cries at me in warning.

'It's alright, girl,' I say to her gently, but then I see her eggs, smashed to pieces. Hatchlings half buried by sand. The tourist kids form a protective half-circle around their destruction.

'Who did this?' I demand. My voice wavers with the rage I am trying to hold tight inside me.

The hot sand burns my feet but I gouge in my toes and wait them out. No honour among them, they jostle him forward. He's about twelve, a dark-haired kid with pale eyes, a future heartbreaker, and he squirms under the weight of the lump of rock he holds up stubbornly like a trophy. His weapon of choice is the size of a brick, sharp-edged and shimmering. Not coastal jetsam. Not flotsam pumice. He's carried this rock down from the quarry, a hundred and sixty-two steps, to murder curlew hatchlings with intent.

My chest goes tight with the cruelty of it. 'Where are your parents?'

'They can kill you,' the egg-thrower says pointing at the mother bird. '*He* said.'

'You're an idiot,' I spit. At sixteen, I can't grapple the injustice of it. 'It's a curlew,' I say. 'And you've killed them.'

I grab the kid still clutching his rock and snarl at the others, 'Bugger off. If I see you back here, I'm going to thump the lot of you.'

As the pack disperses, the bird quiets. I can't bear to watch her approach the nest, to pick through the rubble of eggshell and soft bone. I hold the kid there and make him squirm.

'See what you've done?' I say.

When the curlew takes a chick in her beak and tries to prop it up, I know we've seen enough. I drag him by his bony arm across the hot sand to his parents. He hops and moans, but won't put down the rock. I hope his feet burn. I hope they blister.

'We're from the city,' his mother dares to say, as though the city were void of living things. 'He didn't know.'

Her gold bangles chime as I grab her by the wrist and pour the baby bird into her hand.

'Well, now he knows.'

That night I dream of rising from the sea. Wings spread, feathers dripping. The ocean foaming dark behind me. My call is a song of storms and sorrow.

I wake myself and go down the hall to my brother's room. From the doorway I watch the rise and fall of his sturdy lungs. He sleeps peacefully. He is safe. But I am wide-eyed and turbulent.

The Cape

She comes home late. Not that late, just late enough to make him worry. He says, 'I don't know why you're still following Kane around like he cares about you.'

Dad's not usually like this. He came off his board stupid and sliced his heel. Emma had the car and didn't answer her phone, even though I tried calling her about a million times. We ended up having to get the bus to the clinic and Dad had to stand at the front near the driver because he didn't have any pants to wear, only his wetsuit.

Emma says, 'What happened to your foot?' as she goes into the kitchen to make a start on dinner. I can see the reef-scratches on her back through the thinning cotton of her damp school shirt as she reaches for the dried pasta in the pantry.

'Fin gash,' says Dad. 'What happened to your back?'

'I fell out of a tree' Emma says, not turning around.

Dad raises his eyebrow at me like he hasn't heard this one before. 'Let me guess, Kane told you to climb it?'

'I wasn't with Kane,' she says and her voice shakes with the effort of the lie.

'Then why weren't you answering your phone?'

Emma sighs. 'I'm sorry.' She can't say the rest. She can't say she's been surfing the outer reef with our older brother every day through the summer.

Dad's foot takes yonks to heal. Mostly because he won't stay off it. He insists on coming in the car with us everywhere and hobbling out onto the headland to watch us surf. I don't know if it's Emma or Kane or his foot but something shifts in him those dry weeks while he's landbound.

When he's mended, stitches out, the scar settles into a hard, white lump that hangs off the side of his scrappy Reef sandals.

He hasn't had a surf since. He sits on the bonnet of the car and not even I can corral him into the water. There's always an excuse when someone asks, 'You going out?'

It's never *too big*. It's always something else. Too heavy. Too full. Too onshore.

'Looks like a lot of work for little reward,' he says to me as Emma pulls into an overhead barrel, spray hissing past as the sections close out behind her. My stomach flips with equal parts relief and envy when she makes it out clean.

I know he's not going out because Kane's in the lineup. His orange board is a beacon out there. Always in the prime position for the take-off. Dad used to be better than him. Dad used to be the best surfer among us. Until Kane got sponsored right after mum died and left us too.

'You sure you don't want to come?' I ask, uselessly. I sit with Dad for another five minutes watching bodies get worked by the white-wash.

On the first wave of the next set Kane makes a late drop right off the lip and I can't get out there fast enough to chase a wave like that for myself.

I find Emma out back and say, 'You're on form.'

'I'm getting there.'

A set builds on the horizon and we pull a few strokes further out, not wanting to get caught on the inside.

When we're sitting, the set rolling beneath us, I say, 'I just hope it's worth it.'

Emma says, 'And you're so perfect?'

'I'm just sayin'. Dad doesn't like it.'

'What about you?'

I shrug but tears pinch behind my eyes. 'You've always had a rough go of it – timing the sets going off the rocks.'

'They're short heats. If I want to get to the outer reef at the Cape in time, I have to go off the rocks.' Emma looks past me and adds, 'What happened to Mum was a freak accident.'

'You won't get any points out there,' I say.

'I'm not doing it to win,' she says. 'I'm doing it to get noticed.'

The night before the comp I don't get any sleep. Upstairs I hear Dad pacing on the verandah. When I go outside, he doesn't turn around. He keeps his hands on the railing like he's been expecting me.

'You nervous about tomorrow?'

'Nah,' I shrug. Then, more firmly, 'No.'

'You think your sister's going to go after the big stuff?'

'It's what she likes.'

'She's not ready, you know. She needs to finish school. She's got her whole life ahead of her. Your brother should know better.'

'Kane's an idiot. But Emma's smart. She knows what she's doing.'

'A lot can go wrong out there.'

'Dad,' I say. 'A lot can go wrong anywhere.'

Back in bed, I listen to the ocean driving relentless sets against the headland at the Cape. The sea always sounds louder at night. Closer. More unforgiving. We don't surf the Cape since Mum's gone. It's too hard for Dad to be reminded of her. Of our time together.

I think about Emma asleep with her secrets in the next room. I think about the sand and grit I clean from her new cuts each night after she showers. Her flesh waterlogged. The barnacle-torn skin ragged and white like she has been nibbled by fish. I think about her getting noticed. And sponsored. And leaving us. I think about her being fearless. I think about her being just like Mum.

Emma takes the car early on competition day, eager to warm up with our brother before the blow-ins arrive.

When I arrive on my bike after packing spare towels and Powerade and Tim Tams, Emma and Kane are just small black smudges against the rising green of the outer reef and I know I should be out there with them, closer to Mum.

I pull on my rashie and clamber down the rocks. Holding my board under my arm at awkward angles so I don't bump the nose, fins or tail as I climb down. I wait where the dry rocks become wet for the next set. The first wave shatters to white water and swills around my ankles. In the next moment, Mum always said, there can be no fear. I think of her next to me as the wave builds and crashes onto the rocks, the foam rises. I run, holding my board ahead of me and jump out, landing on the spent wave as it retreats, pulling me with it back to deeper water. I paddle as hard as I can knowing what will happen if I don't. I paddle so fast the rocks and the fear and my sadness are crowded out by my heartbeat raging between my ears. I duck dive under the next breaking wave. And the next. And then I am out in the clear, deep blue. An easy few strokes to the outer bank.

'Hey man,' Kane says. 'Wasn't expecting to see you.' He slaps my shoulder like I'm in on something.

'Where's Emma?' I ask, embarrassed that I'm short of breath. I clamp my mouth shut and try to act casual. Like it's no big deal I'm out back.

Kane stretches on his board, looking back to shore. He's too cool for a rashie or a wetsuit. His ribs are dark with layers of board-rash, the skin scaly like a shedding goanna.

Emma paddles back to us, her face lit up from the last ride.

'Shit,' Emma laughs when she sees me. 'Dad's going to flip.' I think she's going to send me back but all she asks is, 'Did you bring Tim Tams?'

'Back there,' I say, nodding to the shore.

'Let's go then. I'm starved.'

I let Emma and Kane take the first waves of the next set, forgetting that the earlier ones are the smallest. When the next one builds I paddle fast to get out wide on the shoulder and let the wave barrel and hiss and close out behind me, while I ride on my stomach, with nothing to prove, all the way safe to shore.

For the competition, the Cape has turned on a cracking swell, clean and peeling in the early hours and I silently pray to Mum that the wind will stay kind until after the heats. With hot Milo and Tim Tams we watch the production crews setting up tents and stages on the beach below.

'Is Dad coming?' Kane asks.

'Nah,' I say. 'I don't reckon.'

He helps Emma stretch. He repeats statistics to her. He keeps checking the weather on his phone for an update on conditions. Emma smiles through it all, rolls her eyes at me when Kane's not looking. He's got his own heats to worry about, we know. He's doing what Mum used to do for him.

Emma gets a yellow rashie for her heat and we track her all the way out. When the siren sounds, she goes smoothly off the rocks and the commentary goes quiet.

A shadow crosses my beach towel.

'What colour is she?' Dad asks.

'Yellow,' Kane and I say together.

'I can't see her.'

When Kane doesn't, I point past the Cape. 'Out there,' I say.

His shadow shifts. I wish Emma was here because it would be the first time since the funeral we'd all be together. I don't take my eyes off her. She's exactly where she's meant to be.

'Dad,' Kane says. 'She's ready.'

The lunar coast

I was seventeen when the tide went out. I felt it in my lungs. At the height of its run, my breath snared in my chest. I clutched my school shirt as pain seized me.

'Lee, what's wrong?' Alex asked and I saw my agony mirrored in my best mate's eyes.

Alex and I had grown up on the lunar coast. It was a treacherous, northern stretch of coastline with rocky headlands and monstrous tides. Each day the moon peeled away the sea, exposing an atlas of silver sand spits that spiralled into the sea. Our coast protected ships and deterred them.

We were a fishing village that thrived through the winters when the tides were kind and the sun stayed low. Over the summer season of storms, we repaired boats and nets and retold stories of great catches and disasters.

Alex and I loved the summers. The days seemed endless and our fathers stayed home. Though not related, we were a family. Our fathers were boyhood friends. They'd lived off the lunar coast, just as their fathers had done, and we would do. They'd taught us to fish, to read the seas and the stars. We were fourth generation fishermen, or soon would be. The lunar coast was in our blood.

In those summers, salt crunched like gravel at low tide. We'd walk the shoreline, collecting shells and driftwood and sun-bleached bones. We'd roam the rock pools when the weather was right. The rocks scorching from the sun, the water warm to touch. The rock pools were galaxies all of their own, with weeds and crustaceans and fish trapped within. Worlds were interrupted by our touch. We'd catalogue our finds and relay them to our fathers. Our knowledge grew as we did; broadening over the summers.

Alex had the spirit of the sea inside him. Like his father, he was practically made of salt. He was careless in the sun, his shoulders browned to a crisp, his dark hair matted and lips chapped. His feet were broad and tough. I wasn't built for the weather the way he was. To keep up I wore soft-soled reef boots, zinc cream and swimming goggles. My feet were always pale and wrinkled from the wet.

But out there we were equals.

He was always picking things up despite my warnings of stingers and barbs.

'What's this?' he'd ask, running his fingers over a tube anemone, delighted by the way it would suck back in.

In those days, we were ageless. Time melted away only to be revealed in the evening by the extent of our sunburn. We were explorers, pioneers, companions and brothers. Every day was like walking on the moon.

But we did grow up. For so long it felt like it was light years away, then suddenly it was upon us. The rock pools lost their charm. The salt flats seemed less magical. We wanted to take risks, to be challenged and to feel fear.

We found what we were looking for at the headland, where the rocks hollowed out into caverns. There was a vertical, cylindrical cave that went right through the headland. We called it the sea-shuttle.

When the swells were right, we could swim under it and as a wave came in, water would fill the hollow and jettison us to the top. On days with big swells it would almost blow us right into the sky with a whoosh of sea foam and exhilaration.

If we didn't clear the top of the tube, and we rarely did, we would have to grab onto the rocks inside the cave. We had to be swift, and hold strong while the water fell away. If we missed the rocks, and we sometimes did, we'd be sucked out with the swell, tumbled into a whitewash of foam, trapped under the rocks and take water in as breath. While Alex had the courage, I had the lungs and could take two or three rides in a row while he watched enviously from the opening above.

Explaining the cuts on our hands and the scratches on our backs was a nightmare, but the summer was ours and we were delirious with adrenalin. Our fathers would kill us if they knew.

If fishing was the heart of our town, our fishermen were the soul. They were all beanies, whiskers and rubber boots, distinguishable only by the gruffness in their laughs and the kindness in their eyes. We were a superstitious town, like all fishing towns, and Alex and I were regarded with caution, because it was said that our families could feel the sea. Sometimes we believed it, sometimes we didn't. Our fathers' boat was one of the few that operated the nets and the long lines alternately. They relied on the weather to dictate their catch. They were both humble and proud. Like all fishermen, we were slaves to the sea, and sometimes her master.

The night the tide went out, there were big seas. The wind whistled through the weatherboards and Alex and I stayed awake listening to the reports on the radio. Neither of us mentioned the absence of the moon.

At dawn, we went to the ramps; the air was still thick with foam and mist. Our fathers had already returned with an empty hull. In the eerie morning light, I watched them mending the nets. Alex hunched his shoulders against the cold.

'Anything?' I asked.

My father shook his head in that sullen way of his.

Alex's father chuckled his pirate laugh.

'Ah, you can feel it,' he said, pressing his palm to my sternum. Through my jumper I could feel the roughness of his hand. I looked away from the sea, as though my unease was casual, irrelevant.

'You can too, my boy,' he winked at Alex. 'We all can.' He laughed again but there was a sorrow about him.

My father remained silent, but stopped working on his net for a moment and rubbed his own chest, as if irritated by indigestion.

The tide never came back in. Over time, our beach became desolate, shifting from silver to grey, its fine sand becoming pebbled and coarse. The wind stripped the surface revealing craters and debris. In the evenings, as the boats set out, I watched the sea birds circling against the sunset. At night they did not return to our shore.

Each day the fishermen left earlier, with further to sail they combined crews taking fewer boats and more fuel. Our town had retired their nets, relying on the long lines to pull in fish of higher value. Eventually, even they became elusive. It was clear the fish had fled the lunar coast. I couldn't blame them.

When enough days had passed, the boats stopped going out altogether.

'I think it's time we speak seriously about your future,' my mother said over dinner of tinned tuna. I'd been set to start my apprenticeship with Alex on our fathers' boat in autumn.

'We were worried something like this would happen,' my father said, not looking at me.

'I know…' I pushed the flakes around my plate. 'I'll go.'

I left for college the following month. Alex didn't even say goodbye.

It was six years before I returned to the lunar coast.

Our town had changed dramatically. The boats had all been hauled ashore and lay tilted unsettlingly on the banks, their keels exposed. The ocean-front stores, once hardware and bait shops, now sold ice creams and sunhats.

My parents, had opened a small bakery there and now my mother smelt of pastry. Her hair had grown long and she kept it tied up in a messy knot. I couldn't help noticing she smiled more.

My father sat with Alex's father on our patio, watching the sun bake the beach. I was overjoyed to see them together, despite knowing how his spirit had dried up like the sea.

I'd heard from old friends that Alex had taken a job as a tour guide, driving the coast, pointing out nail-tail wallabies in the spinifex.

As I sat, my father squeezed my shoulder with his large brown hand.

'Seen him?' he asked.

'Not yet.'

'You should.'

'I know.'

I met with Alex cautiously at first, over a beer at the tavern, then for dinner with his family. Eventually, we began to spend the days together.

A week after our first reunion, we drove his company 4-wheel-drive to the point. We'd only ever walked the coast, but now the distance seemed too far to contemplate.

'Dad said you wouldn't come back until the tide turned,' he said finally, as though the ocean had brought me back, not my family, and not him.

'Has it?'

He said nothing for a while, then smiled. 'I think so.'

We parked on the beach then climbed the head-land, the rocks were brittle, leaving powder on my knees and hands. At the top, I looked out over the coast.

'Well?' Alex asked with laboured breath.

'I think you're right.'

The sea was coming back. We watched it for some time, awed, as it rolled back in carrying dried weed and wood, drowning the sand. And then, just a few metres out, that unmistakable flash in the water. There, and there again.

'Did you see that?' I pointed and Alex followed my gaze.

'It can't be…'

We raced to the beach and peeled off our clothes. We had to get a closer look. Among all the salt and the sunburnt kelp there were fish. No doubt about it.

'Come on,' he hurried me, as I pulled on my boots. While he had never mocked me before, he did now.

'What is all this stuff anyway?' he snatched at my diving mask and my towel laughing in the cruel way of a teenager made desperate by age.

I was just another city boy to him now. Our history had fallen with the tide, erased by the time and the distance I'd put between us.

Despite his cruelty, or because of it, I pitied him. Life on the lunar coast had him beat. I was fitter than I had ever been, yet he had developed a paunch. His body sagged in a way I had never imagined it could. Time had been fierce to him.

We entered the water. I waded to my chest, before diving in. The water was murky with salt. It flooded my mouth, swelling my tongue. I could hardly see even through my mask. When I looked back at Alex, he had his eyes squeezed shut.

At the headland we bobbed on the surface. The wind had picked up, chopping the water into messy white caps.

'Did you see it?' he asked.

'No.' I spat into the water.

'I think we should check the shuttle.'

I'd forgotten all about it.

We rounded the headland and were fully exposed to the wind. The tide was rushing in, as though making up for lost time after half a decade of slack water. It had already moved more than a metre.

I'd expected this landscape to be foreign to me, but as I swam, I felt my body guided by the sea.

With familiar strokes I pushed under the surface and into the opening.

I broke the surface and gasped, holding tight to the rocks. It had been a rough swim, the visibility making it nearly impossible to navigate in the hollow. Still, Alex came up grinning.

'Grab the rocks,' I said leading him to the wall. 'I can hardly see anything.' We were in a washing machine. The surface churned with foam.

'It's down there,' he said with certainty.

'Did you see it?' My back scraped the rocks as I rose with the next surge of water.

'No, but I feel it.'

'We'll climb out and have another look.'

'We don't have time for that.'

'I just wanted to know what kind it was.'

'Lee, we can't let it get away!' He smiled devilishly before letting go of the rock.

'Alex!' I grabbed at his wrist but he slipped free.

I waited for him to resurface. I calculated the climb to the top. It was just a few metres. I reminded myself I'd done it hundreds of times. I counted to ten. Alex still wasn't back. Shit.

He'd played tricks like this before, pretend there was a giant squid dragging him under then take hold of my ankle. Or he'd come back up with a handful of sand to rub in my hair. This felt different from those times.

I put my face in the water. Nothing. I kicked out with my feet hoping to brush something other than rock. I looked again. It was like swimming in storm clouds. I couldn't see anything.

I took a deep breath and let go of the rocks.

My body plunged into the darkness. I was surrounded by bubbles and foam. Down I went, trusting my memory of the passage. My hands stretched out feeling nothing but water and rock. I kicked against another surge, I had to stay down until I found him. I felt the pressure on my lungs but knew I could beat it. I reached again, hitting the sand with my shoulder. And then, flesh! I grabbed Alex with both hands and pulled him towards me.

I dragged Alex up the lunar coast and lay him on his side. Was he breathing? I pulled off my mask and held my ear to his face. I felt the steady thud of his heart under my hand, his breath on my cheek. I stood up and gulped down my own lungful of precious air. I watched the rise and fall of my still-pale chest. I looked at my skinny ankles in my boots. I was dripping, exhausted, alive.

So was Alex.

Only then did I notice the fish clawed in his hand. As though coming out of a coma, it began to flap on the sand, its body contorting, frantic, feeble. I knew then why he'd gone back down. This fish, the first to return, was the one thing that could restore him. To catch it would make him a fisherman after all these wasted years.

But the fish needed to be in the sea if we had any hope for the lunar coast. It needed to be alive. I bent to pry it from his grasp, but Alex sprung awake. His eyes jolted open, he looked from me to the fish, first confused then ecstatic with pride. He raised himself on one elbow, leering at the fish on the sand. With his free hand he grabbed hold of my mask and punched down with all his strength.

When the mask crushed the fish's skull, I felt it in my lungs.

Tell-tale

I see Maggie through the window before she sees me. She's still waking up. The strap on her singlet has fallen off her shoulder but she ignores it as she moves about the kitchen. She's making bread while still lucid, baking in a dream-state. Gathering and mixing the ingredients with heavy eyelids and messy hair.

Her delivered newspaper has been tossed up onto the patio and I scoop it up and tap on the glass. She looks up, her face alighting with recognition.

'It's open,' she says. I imagine the sound of the words coming off her lips rather than really hearing them.

I push open the door and go in.

'So, you got a story in this one?' she asks as I take a seat at the bench and unfurl the paper. She gives me her whole attention and it is warm and familiar.

'It's no big deal,' I say, but after pushing for lines for the better part of the year, we both know I'm lying.

'Ha.' Her laugh is triumphant. 'Let's see it.'

The story is barely a hundred words, hidden back on page sixteen, under an ad for the local butcher. I push the paper toward her and watch her read, leaning over the counter holding her floured fingers in the air, arms bent at the elbows like a nurse.

After a minute she makes an airy, dissatisfied sound. 'Your name's not on it.'

'I'm still new,' I say, hating the way it sounds coming out.

She gives me a look I can't read, and just like that, Maggie is back to the business of her morning. She goes to the sink and turns on the tap with her elbows and begins washing the flour from her hands.

'It doesn't matter that you're new, Tom,' she says with her back to me. 'You just have to want it more.' She flicks the water from her fingers, turns off the tap and finishes drying her hands on her jeans. 'What's on the cover?' she asks.

I slap the pages closed and feel my heart drop. The cover story isn't a story at all. Maggie leans in to read the headline. I can't look her in the eye.

When the oven timer pings it startles us both. I fold the paper in half to hide the embarrassment on the front page. Maggie goes to the oven, scratching the back of her ear, her arm is muscular and beautiful and I wonder if I'll ever stop loving her. She swaps the trays, removing the baked bread and sliding in the newly-rested dough.

She brings the fresh bread to the bench and says, about the cover, 'Who thought that would be a good idea?'

I can't admit to her the cover is my mistake.

As she shakes the loaf from the tin, turning it out onto the rack to cool, something rights itself. Now that the bread is ready, a barrier of normalcy has been restored. I could go back outside and come back in like any other morning. Pulling open the glass door, with the smell of fresh bread, it could be any day. But it's this one.

Our town is so small everyone knows each other's business. We gossip and speculate about our families, neighbours and friends. In our town, news travels with or without the help of the local rag. So some weren't surprised when the details of a resident's personal mail ended up printed on the front page of our stalwart *Navigator*.

See, we don't have a mail delivery service, only a hole-in-the-wall Post Office with a bank of pigeon holes. Things get shoved in and moved and misplaced. It's not uncommon for a bill for the box above or below or beside yours to end up with your lot. There's always a gaggle of people cramped around the boxes shuffling through their wad of mail and re-shelving stray letters before leaving. I do it too, usually. Just not yesterday. Yesterday I grabbed the mail from the *Navigator's* pigeonhole and rushed back to work, leaving the stack of letters on my desk and one of them, not addressed to the *Navigator* at all, was printed on the front page overnight. Now the whole town knows Mr Richards has listed his beachfront penthouse for sale for $1.2 million, even though the property evaluation came back for half that amount.

As a newsprint journalist, perhaps I shouldn't be rushing round on my bicycle collecting the mail anyway? Well, I'm not exactly considered a newsprint journalist around here. After four years at university in the city, I'm back in my hometown writing advertorials for the *Navigator*. Hardly living the dream, as Maggie likes to remind me.

Not that she's doing so great herself.

She's half way through two abandoned online courses and works most days at the grease shop on the Esplanade before heading up to the tavern to pull beers at night.

When she got the job that first summer, she'd go in early to use the industrial ovens. She'd bake until the store opened, and give away her treats to the tourists ordering their fish and chips. The tourists gorged themselves on fruit-mince pies, biscuits and pastries. Then she started making her own breads, loaves and sticks and rolls fresh from the oven each morning. She ignored the crates of plastic-wrapped sugar rolls – white death she called them – and instead filled her own creations with fish and meat and salad made to order. The hungry locals lurked across the Esplanade, unsure of queue the coiled out the door and down the street. Wasn't she just a barmaid? At 2pm each day she'd clock-off at the shop and swap her pale blue apron for a black one and walk two streets up to the tavern to begin her shift there. That summer she worked on her feet until her toenails fell off. And she wouldn't have changed anything for the world. The shop was bought out by a big-city investor the next summer. 'Why would you give away food?' he'd said, allegedly. 'Stick to what we're here for. If it's not on the menu, don't sell it.' That was that. Back she went to serving up deep fried foods, stale ham rolls, and icy poles. So much for her dream, too.

From Maggie's, I don't go to the office. I don't even call in sick. Instead I go home and pace the pathetic perimeter of my lawn wondering what to do next, how to make it right. The grass is crunchy underfoot. My toes flex away from the heat of the mineral sand. There's always been more sand than grass in my yard but today it's particularly insulting. As if a mortgage at twenty-two wasn't the worst idea in the world. It was also wasted on an oceanfront asbestos shack that would never good enough for Maggie.

At a loss, I ride my bike up to the headland to check the surf. The cars are accusingly slow as they drive past me. I haven't played hooky since high school but there's a familiar thrill to it. Adrenalin flushes away some of my guilt as I pick up speed toward the headland. By the time I slide into the lookout carpark, my heart is pumping hard in my chest and I almost feel right again. I leave my bike and walk out to the lookout that hangs over the water. In school, guys would bring their girls up here and romance them with the move from the *Titanic* movie. I'd never tried it. The only girl wanted in high school was Maggie.

There are a few guys out in the water below and I lean on the railing, resting my chin on my hands while I watch. The salt air begins to work itself into my lungs. My shoulders relax. I run verbs through my head watching the surfers, always practising how I'd describe the waves if I ever got the chance to write about them. Maggie was right. I don't want the newspaper gig enough. I don't want it at all. I never did. It was meant to be a stepping stone, by way of sports writing, into a job at *Coast* magazine. I'd interned at *Coast* back when I was still at uni. The editor then was a true master of his art, who suggested I needed a bit more life experience before joining the team, thus the job at the *Navigator*, which was obviously working out so well.

When the Ed retired, the job was passed down to his editorial assistant Andy Milne, a wannabe, a failed pro surfer who thought writing and making money was the same thing. The magazine had suffered because of it. I was still trying to find my way back in. This was what I wanted to write about. The sea, the sport, the survival of human v. nature. This.

Gravel crunches behind me and I turn to see Andy Milne and his entourage crowd into the lookout. Great. Perfect.

'Hey,' Andy says, coming to lean on the railing next to me. 'It's Tim, yeah?'

'Tom,' I say, keeping my eyes on the water.

'RDO?'

'Something like that.'

'What's going on at that paper of yours, mate? Up to something?'

I want to disappear inside my t-shirt. 'I dunno,' I say. 'Something.'

'Well, it's certainly got my attention.'

He waits for me to respond but I have nothing to say. Attention isn't always a good thing.

I push back from the railing but Andy grabs my arm.

'I've got these work experience groms in this week. We're doing the usual. A trip out to Big Chiefs to see a Billabong billboard being made, then out to the web-press. You wouldn't be interested in tagging along?'

'Why?' I say, sensing a trap.

He laughs. 'Why not?'

'I'll think about it.'

'Tom … Don't worry too much about this mail business. Think of it as publicity. It will be great for revenue.'

'Sure,' I say and turn my back on him.

'See you tomorrow,' he calls, like he owns me. His entourage sees me off with a round of applause.

The convenience store where Maggie works is one of the oldest shopfronts on the esplanade. Set in the front rooms of a small cottage, the shop faces the sea claiming enviable real estate with big windows facing the Pacific, and an airy porch busy with flaking patio furniture and hanging planters spilling pigface.

When I arrive to the shop, the chairs are still stacked on the patio and the door is closed. Not for the first time, I unstack the chairs for Maggie, slapping them into formation around the tables. Then I pick the cigarette butts out from between the floorboards and press my finger into the dry dirt of the pot plants. Like me, the plants could use a drink.

When I try the handle, the door is still locked. Finally, I notice a handwritten message on a pie bag taped in the window: *back in 5 minutes xo*. I go down the side of the cottage looking for the hose and hear voices at the end of the alleyway. I push past the wheelie bins into the backyard, where Maggie is smoking a cartoonishly thin cigarette and chatting to her delivery driver. He has both hands in his pockets and is wearing an expression like a spooked horse.

'Hey man,' I say. *Easy*. To Maggie I gesture to the back door and ask, 'Is it open?'

Maggie covers one hand delicately over the other, masking the already-seen cigarette from me. 'Why wouldn't it be?'

The trolley of bread rolls and tinned fruit is parked at the door. I lift a slab of pineapple slices under my arm and go in through the screen. A few years ago, she would have been sneaking out on her shifts from the tavern to chat me up.

Inside, I turn on all the lights in the shop front and start up the till.

Maggie comes to the door, holding the cigarette at arm's length.

'You OK?' she asks.

'Are you smoking again?'

'Just this one.'

'Gross,' I say.

'You are.'

I don't want to play this game with her today. There are moments when I think we could be unsinkable. And others, like this one, when I think loving Maggie is the greatest disaster of all time.

'You sure you're OK?' she asks again

'Why wouldn't I be?' I say, refusing to let her pull me under. I unlock the front door and go out, pulling down her stupid sign on the way. Then I ride my bike across town to the *Coast* office.

The following Tuesday when a court summons runs on the front page I hand in my resignation at the *Navigator* and take up at *Coast* five days a week, unpaid, as Andy Milne's assistant. It's not a writing job. It's not even a job, really. But after driving his work experience kids around, talking at them about printing and advertising for a whole day, I realise the only way to get a job at *Coast* was the same way you did with anything in the surf industry: by hanging around, or having a hot younger sister. And I don't have the latter.

As far as bosses go, Andy is OK, and the gig is easy enough. I spend the hours sending sponsorship requests, I test products that arrive to the office for advertorials, and write letters to the magazine posing as loyal Coast readers. I'm told my goal is to generate revenue. Though, mostly, and more importantly, I have the ongoing duty of texting his wife.

For authenticity, he has a style guide. When to use capital letters, which emoticon he prefers to use to represent a smiley face, how many minutes to wait before responding. Andy himself doesn't seem that busy, but as the days pass, I come to understand the relentlessness of Mrs Milne.

'Your wife wants to know if you want to take red or white wine to … J&H's on the weekend?'

'Red.'

'She says… they're serving fish.'

'White then.'

'She says she loves you,' I put the phone down and resume stacking blocks of wax on Andy's freebie shelf. 'Couldn't she just decide herself?'

'Of course she could,' Andy says without looking up. 'Marriage is a compromise, Tom.'

On Tuesday, the *Navigator* runs a piece of mail addressed to Maggie's mum about her increasing medical debt for cosmetic surgery and Maggie finally calls me. I'm downstairs in the archives looking for a back issue of *Coast* that had Kelly Slater and Cameron Diaz on the cover that we can photograph again instead of paying for the image reprint rights. I haven't seen the latest edition of the newspaper, but I've heard about it.

'Why didn't you stop this?' Maggie demands before I get a chance to say hello.

'I quit the *Navigator*.'

'When?'

'Last week,' I say, the phone pressed between my shoulder and my ear as I rummage.

'Oh,' Maggie says. 'So you didn't know they were running this?'

I straighten up. 'Is your mum OK?'

'She'll be OK. She's just so embarrassed.' Maggie exhales loudly into the phone. Then she says, 'Hey, you know what, I've got Friday off and I've met someone you'll like. Let's go out.'

'Sure,' I say, wondering if she'll pull the dagger out herself or leave it in to twist on Friday.

On Friday night, after three beers at home, I'm finally ready to go out to meet Maggie. I ride my bike the long way to the tavern, slogging up to the headland and coasting down the road on the other side, heart pounding, wind flushing the fear from me.

As the only watering hole in town, the tavern is packed and I have to push my way through to find Maggie. She is near the back windows, guarding two seats.

'Where's your friend?' I ask.

She leans in and kisses me. Her lips lingering soft on my cheek.

'Bathroom,' she says. Then, squeezing my hand, 'I've *missed* you.'

'Have you?' I ask.

'You sit here, save our seats. I'll get us drinks.'

Before I can protest, she's off, slicing through the crowd with her narrow waist in skinny black jeans.

I sit, and wait, resisting the urge to get out my phone. I've never been a gadget guy, but all of the work for Andy is habit forming. I was getting used to being in demand. Or, at least, getting used to being Andy.

'Excuse me?'

I look up to see a knockout blonde, a couple of years older, peering at me.

'You're in our seats,' she says, placing her hand on her hip for emphasis.

'I don't think so,' I say.

She makes her lips a hard, thin line. 'You are.'

I haven't lost all my journalistic skills just yet. '*You're* Maggie's friend?'

Her expression transforms before me. 'Tom?' she says with relief. 'Too funny! I'm Cate. Maggie has told me everything about you. Well, not everything,' she corrects herself. 'She's told me you're a writer for the *Navigator*. What's that like?'

Maggie returns holding a tray of drinks above her head like a pro. 'Oh good, you've met,' she says, setting the drinks on the window sill.

'Tom was just telling me what it's like to ruin people's lives.'

Even Cate's anger is captivating.

'Actually,' I say. 'I left the *Navigator*. I'm doing a bit with *Coast* now.'

'*Really?*' Cate and Maggie ask in unison.

'Really.'

Cate brushes her hair away from her face. 'My husband works there. You might know him. He's the editor. Well, that's what he says he is. Bit of a con, I reckon.' She laughs, not cruelly, but with a breath of malice I can't ignore.

'I don't know what he does in there all day. He texts me every five minutes. Always wants to know what I'm doing. Won't let me make a decision on my own.'

'Red or white?' I say before I can stop myself.

'Exactly,' Cate says. 'I married him because I thought he was this hot-shot writer. I thought he had passion and integrity and wanted to, I don't know, *change things*. Now all I hear about is sponsorship deals and cost-savings and ad-space sales and…' Cate waves her arm looking for the word.

'Revenue?' I offer.

She looks me right in the eyes, 'Yes!' She clinks her class against mine so hard I fear they might smash in our hands.

'You know what, Tom,' she says. 'I feel like I already know you.'

Over drinks, Maggie tells me she met Cate at a wellness retreat.

'It was all about future-proofing your emotions,' Cate says. 'Or some nonsense. I just needed a few days peace.'

'I got a lot out of it,' Maggie says meekly. She's beige beside Cate, like her lights have been dimmed.

'Enough about us.' Cate turns her attention on me like the sweep of a lighthouse. 'Tell me, Tom. What's on your front page?'

Maggie sips her drink. She knows she's my front page. Maybe I should just say it. Instead, I turn the question back on Cate.

'Oh, it's boring, really,' she waves me away for show while happily enjoying the spotlight. 'I'm leaving my husband, if you must know. Or he's leaving me. I haven't worked out the details on *how* yet but the *what* is me keeping the house and him leaving town.'

Maggie drains her drink while possibility, or maybe, hope, billows in my gut. Imagine *Coast* without Andy. Imagine Cate without Andy. I finish my own drink to flood the feelings.

Cate sees right through me. 'You think that might be good for you?'

Beside me, Maggie tenses. I wonder if she can see Cate without Andy, too.

Later, outside the tavern, a cool breeze blows off the ocean. The streets are empty. All the cabs have gone, full of passengers, out to the suburbs and I know it will be ages until they turn back in. We wait with Cate on the Esplanade for her taxi to arrive. The booze has loosened us and I let the sea-breeze sway me so my shoulder bumps the cool of Maggie's skin. There's a glow in her cheeks like she's holding in a secret.

'Maybe Andy can get you?' I suggest to Cate.

'He's not texting me back,' she says, looking at the dark screen of her phone.

'We can all go to Tom's place,' Maggie offers. 'It's close. And right on the beach.'

I'm about to protest, just as the taxi pulls into the street.

After Cate gets in and the cab sets sail for her home, Maggie turns to me and says, 'Maybe we can still go to your place?'

'I have a better idea,' I say.

Perched on my handlebars, I double Maggie up to the lookout. It's slow going and after six beers I'm wobbling all over the place. I think it's the magic of Maggie, and pride, keeping me upright.

I'm a sweaty mess when we get to the top but by some miracle, the lookout is empty. Maggie does her best graceful dismount and we're both laughing against the wind as we go out to the railing. The Pacific is a glorious, undulating black.

Maggie grips the rail with both hands, leaning out over the ocean, she inhales deeply. I know if I speak, I'll ruin everything. So instead I stand behind her, place my hands over hers.

'Tom,' she says, laughing quietly. 'I trust you.'

I bring our hands from the railing and stretch them out wide. The salt wind and night air and every possibility rushing against us.

The Breakers

We are armpit deep in the Pacific when I tell him I have left you. You are living with your uncle under some arrangement I don't want to know about. But there have been northerlies for a month and the onshore winds kept bringing in the stingers; so even though you are gone, I have not told my father.

I don't know what I expected out there in the gentle, two-foot swell. Something more human, I guess. Something that told me I'd done the right thing. Sou'easter now or not, perhaps I was expecting too much from him.

When I say nothing happened, my father laughs, 'You don't expect me to believe that?'

He's misunderstood me, but I swallow my rebuttal like a gulp of seawater and he catches another wave all the way to the shore, even though we are between the sets.

When he swims back to me he is out of breath and if he has any advice, he doesn't offer it. We turn our backs on the shore and watch the horizon.

'It was just time, you know?'

'I know,' he says.

And we leave it there. Five years reduced to a few sentences on an outgoing tide. He understands time, as do I.

These days I worry about his lungs. His chest heaves with breathlessness when we swim, and he is greyer somehow. There will be a day when I am stronger than him, but even then, there will be things we won't say, regardless of the time and the tide that is running out between us.

All Hands

Of course she was swimming. Out beyond the lagoon, past the sandbar where the Pacific threw dumpers at the shallows, her elbows made vicious points with each stroke. She swam with an unnatural crawl, a testament to her determination. Learning to swim fifty years too late didn't mean a damn thing. Now, finally, she loved being in that ocean.

Anxiety turned my words to mush in my gut as I waited for her to come to shore. I was desperate to explain. I owed her that much. I'd been gone for six years. As I watched her make her turn at the mouth of the lagoon and begin stroking back, I knew I couldn't wait a moment longer. I had to get in. Get it over with.

I pulled my shirt over my head and yanked off my jeans. The denim stuck to the nervous sweat on my clammy calves as I struggled out of them. Then I rushed the shore.

The lagoon swallowed me up. Feet, shins, knees, thighs. The early glare shimmered gold off the surface. I waded to the sandbar and pushed through the breakers. The waves tugged mockingly at the loose elastic of my jocks.

Once clear of the dumpers, I saw her. Out the back. Waiting for me. She was up to her shoulders, wearing the Pacific like a shawl, her body threaded into a black Speedo cat-suit. All jutting bones and loose skin. Her collarbone too distinct, her hair grey against the morning light.

'When did you get back?' she said.

'Mum,' I said. 'It's Rebecca…'

'She's dead?'

I tried to ignore the hope in her voice. 'No,' I said. 'She's left me.'

My parents built their house from scratch, literally using their bare hands. They constructed the house on a block dismissed by everyone as being too close to the ocean, too susceptible to the southerly wrath. They'd worked on the house every weekend over a year, calling in favours from all the tradespeople and mates that they knew. They pooled tools and beers and man-hours until the house was complete. Ultimate beachfront and no neighbours in sight. Their house was magnificent, too. It wasn't some hodgepodge seaside shanty. My parents were true products of DIY culture, back before punk made DIY cool again. Dad is a builder and Mum was a nurse. Whenever I'm suffering a crisis of confidence, my favourite game is to stack myself up against the two people who can pretty much make, mend, heal or create anything. I guarantee it: without even trying, my parents constantly put me to shame. With Rebecca gone, I'd been having these thoughts more and more. Enough to finally make me get in my car and come back here to face them again.

Back from the swim, Mum let me shower first in her new ambulant bathroom. The glass on the shower screen was so clean I didn't believe her when she said the reno had been done almost two years ago. I showered cautiously, keeping my elbows close, sluicing the shampoo foam from the glass before drying myself off.

As I dressed in my old bedroom, I couldn't recognise the space. All of my things were packed into sealed plastic tubs and stacked in the wardrobe. The room had been white washed and decorated like something from a magazine on Hamptons style.

'You've done some work,' I said, joining Mum on the verandah. She'd made Mocconas and had a jar of monkey biscuits on the table. I sipped the coffee and was comforted by its simplicity. It hadn't been made with frothed low-cal milk by a hipster barista, nor had it come from an ocean-clogging plastic pod. Just hot, simple, coffee.

'You like the room?' Mum asked.

'Yeah,' I said. 'It's very…'

She set her mug on the table. 'What?'

'*What* yourself? I like it,' I lied, feeling utterly displaced.

She knew what I wasn't saying. She let a moment pass then replied, 'You're almost thirty, Ben.'

She was right. I was almost thirty. And this hadn't been my home for years. For the past six, I'd been doing FIFO. My fly-in was to Moranbah and my fly-out was to Rebecca in Melbourne. Rebecca didn't have the same love of the coast as I did and even though she endured our frequent Saturday trips to the muddy excuse of a beach at St Kilda in our early days, I longed for something more. Torquey? Bells? Rebecca wouldn't hear of it. Eventually, I quit on the St Kilda trips as well. That was the problem with Rebecca. She vacuumed the *me-ness* from me, until I was a just a boring, bulked-up piece of arm-candy with no opinions of my own. And then she was done with me.

Home for me, pre-Rebecca, was a low-set fibro beach shack a few hours north, up the coast from my parents. The best I could find with what I could afford was a hodgepodge seaside shanty two streets back from the ocean. An investment opportunity paid for with dirty coal money. I never thought it would be an investment I'd need to cash in on.

After selling up, I had little left for rent. So I was back, edging my way back in to the empty nest.

Dad arrived home after dark. The truck, boat and trailer rumbled up over the drive. It took him a few more attempts than I remembered, trying to reverse it into the carport. After dinner, and two bottles of shiraz shared between the three of us, Dad finally loosened up. I watched it come over him. The day melted away.

'Well, what now?' he said.

'Gary,' Mum chided, her mouth purple from the wine.

'It's fine,' I said, calmly. 'It's a good question.'

'You getting any compo from her?'

'Compo?'

'A payout.'

'It's not like I've been terminated unfairly, Dad. Besides, we're not divorced. Just … separating.'

'Oh,' Mum said. She raised her glass with both hands, as though trying to hide behind it.

Dad cleared his throat. 'But she still makes good money, doing what she does? What's it called again?'

'Derivatives?' I offered.

'Derivatives,' Dad said nodding. 'And if you got divorced, you'd get half?'

'Theoretically,' I shrugged.

Squinting at me, Dad added, 'So what are you going to do now?'

This was dangerous territory. They knew I'd been exiled from FIFO in the last round of cuts. What they didn't know was that since then, for six months, I'd been a kept man. A trophy husband. My job was to look good at networking events, schmooze philanthropists, keep my nose clean. A tough gig. And then Rebecca had a gut-full of me and told me to get out.

Since then, I'd been selling up. The Sunny Coast house, and all the useless shit I'd accumulated while off-shift. All the things I'd bought while battling loneliness at the camp, one MasterCard transaction at a time. Six years of my life was now available on Gumtree. If you could call jet skis and golf-clubs and signed Wallabies jerseys a *life*. These possessions had come from the internet in dark times, and in darker times I was sending them back again.

Dad slopped the last of the wine into his glass and held the bottle bottom-up until the last drop dripped in. I could tell he wasn't in the mood for sharing.

'I'm running an online business, actually.'

Dad looked at Mum, then to me he said, 'I don't trust the Cloud.' After a few days at home, my sister Shelley finally returned my calls. She was younger, but not by much, an accomplished architect and one of those straight-up, beer-drinking, footy-watching women who could still tell you the difference between a Blahnik and a Choo.

She phoned from her Mazda 9, on speaker phone, while running errands.

'Lousy bitch,' Shelley said, barely audible over the howl of her two step-kids in the backseat behind her.

'Have you seen the house?' I asked, to change the subject.

'Hayden, *stop*.' The delivery of the command to her rat-pack silenced me as well. 'Of course they've made changes, Ben. They're not spring chickens anymore.'

'So, you have seen it?'

She almost snorted. 'Seriously?'

I'd been home for almost a week but it was my sister's derision that finally made me realise I'd been time-travelling. Somehow, I'd thought my sojourn West and my one-week-a-month devotion to an all-consuming Victorian romance meant everything I'd left behind, everything I'd been flying in from, would stand still. I was wrong, of course. In six years, everything: my sister, my parents, the house; all had moved forward. Only I was stuck in the past. I'd been transplanted, older, more worn out, back to a life I should have graduated from when I left high school. Dad was right. What was I going to do now?

'Was she cheating?' Shelley asked.

'What? No. *She* left *me.*'

'Were you cheating?'

'No.'

'Then what? What did you do to stuff up the only good thing in your life?'

'Nothing,' I said, which was probably, if I really thought about it, true.

'Here, talk to your uncle, Hayden,' my sister said handing the phone to my snot-nosed step-nephew. 'Talk soon, love you,' she said before the kid started up.

Mum filled her days well. She had a routine that was both busy and luxurious. Her swim in the morning after Dad left for work was followed by a brunch of fruit, tea and toast on the patio. Then she filled the bird baths, put out seed for the lorikeets and spent some time in the garden. Chores followed – these were different day to day:

laundry, cleaning, baking, sewing buttons back onto Dad's work shirts. By lunch, she worked on renovation drawings on a huge architect desk – probably a hand-me-down from Shelley – that they'd installed in Shelley's old room facing the windows that looked out over the scrubby bush. Or she watched snippets of TV home makeover shows, or flicked through style magazines and clipped out the images that interested her.

I tried to occupy myself with scraps of Dad's western novels, but more often than not found myself hovering.

'Go into the garden,' she said. 'Do something.'

This was the problem. I couldn't *do* anything. I didn't have hands like theirs.

In the mornings, with Dad off to work and Mum swimming laps of the lagoon, the house seemed big and vacant. I didn't like being left with my thoughts too long, so I began to join her at the beach. At first, I just watched from the shore, walking lengths of the beach like a mournful dog-owner. I'd packed poorly for the visit home, bringing all my stupid fancy southerner clothes instead of thongs, shorts and tees. Autumn or not, it was beach weather. Mum sorted me out by running up some elastic-waisted board shorts on her old Singer. They were Baywatch-red and somehow flattering, a splash of colour against the sea's blue and the beige of my mood.

At first, I couldn't keep up with Mum, my lungs were unused to the whole-body exertion against the swell. Sure, I worked out. I was gym-fit. Selfie-fit. I wore my muscles in the right places. That didn't mean I was sea-faring. The coast demanded a kind of body I didn't have. One that was sun-hardened, ready for life.

I swam with Mum every day. My lungs conditioned quickly, responding to the challenge of becoming an ocean swimmer again.

Toward the end of the second week home, after our swim as we came across the sand, Mum seemed slower. I offered her my elbow for support and for once, she took it.

'My joints,' she said. She was older than I remembered. When she touched my arm, her skin had taken on the cold from the ocean. I helped her from the beach up onto the boardwalk through the tea trees to the house. Mum stopped at the end of boardwalk before navigating the few steps down to the lawn and said, 'I wanted to ask about your house.'

'OK,' I said cautiously. The salt was drying tight and sticky on my skin.

'Are you sure you want to sell it?'

'What do you mean?'

'You don't think you can work it out with her?'

I shrugged, lip out like a sulking teenager. 'She doesn't want to be with me anymore. I think I just need to be here a little while.'

She looked at the house, then to me, her face softer, almost apologetic. She said, 'You know, I've never known with you how long *a little while* really is.'

'What's that supposed to mean?' I said, defensively.

She breathed out slowly. 'Ben, you can't hide here forever.'

Dad had different habits. He worked from dawn, rattling down the driveway in his ute, sometimes with the boat in tow if he had other trades in and could sneak out for a fish through lunch. When he got home, he would be straight in to some other project, working on the garden with Mum, tinkering in the shed fixing things that you could buy new cheaper than the cost of the glue needed to make the repair. He cleaned gutters, filleted fish, chopped wood for the barbeque, or took Mum back to the beach for another swim, though their afternoon swims were far more leisurely. Some days I could only track him by the trail of his clothes. He seemed to move through the house shedding his hi-vis work uniform like a second skin.

On Friday night, we sat up together, drinking rum, each pour taking us to the top of the next B on the Bundaberg bottle. Between us, the table was strewn with tackle. Occupying his hands seemed to be the only way he knew how to talk. It had always been impossible to just have a conversation. To have a conversation over a game of darts or hand of cards, or while fishing, or gardening, or peeling potatoes was the most natural thing for him. Rigging the traces for whiting lines wasn't a bad way to spend a Friday night. There was memory and comfort in the repetition of the work. Hook, red bead, trace, swivel. Wrapping them in rows around square scraps of coolite.

By the time we were halfway down the Bundy label, Dad's pocket vibrated. He pushed his glasses back up his nose, looked at the screen.

'Huh,' he said, almost surprised. Then he scraped his chair back and took the call outside.

'Who was calling you so late?' I asked when he came back to the table.

He looked at the clock and I followed his eyes, embarrassed to see it was only eight thirty.

'Rebecca,' he said. He picked up the line he'd been working on, threaded his knot and pulled it tight between his teeth.

'What is she calling you for?'

He finished with the trace and began coiling it neatly around the block. When he was finished, he put the block into the tackle box, and looked at me.

'Because we're family,' he said.

I blinked at him. 'She calls you often?'

'Not too often.'

'Did she ask about me?'

He selected another hook and tested the rusting tip against the pad of his thumb.

'She asked if it was a good time to be buying mulloway.'

The Saturday fish market was a ritual of ours. I realised I'd made the same mistake again. Like my parents' life, Rebecca's was going on without me.

'And what did you tell her?'

Dad sipped his rum. The ice clinked against the side of his glass. 'I told her maybe she should ask her husband.'

My sister arrived on Saturday morning, a kid under each arm and her Dior sunnies pushed up on top of her head, holding back her wavy brown hair as she wrestled everyone out of the car.

'Take him,' she said, jutting her hip so Hayden, the eldest, slipped from her and I had no choice but to catch him. Parenting, Shelly had told me, was the most physical and tactical sport of all. It was all defensive plays, counterattacks, blocks, scrummages, and, if she was lucky, the occasional victory.

'Don't you wanna walk, big man?' I said to Hayden encouragingly. As I lowered him to the ground he wailed and my sister shot me her classic I-told-you-so look. I settled him onto my hip and helped her with her bags with my free hand.

The little one, River, hid behind Shelley's hair.

'I didn't know you were coming.'

Shelley kissed my cheek. 'And miss your grand meltdown? Are you kidding?'

'Thanks,' I said.

'And you know,' she added, more serious. 'It's all hands when there's trouble.'

We took the boat out after lunch. Six of us crammed in under the Bimini top. Hayden yanked at the clips on his tiny life-vest and River sat quietly on Dad's knee, co-captaining us to the fishing grounds.

Shelley wore white linen shorts and a scarf around her hair. Her huge sunnies making her look like she belonged on a yacht in the Riviera. I was wearing one of Dad's too-big t-shirts and it flapped wildly in the wind.

Shelley slapped my stomach with the back of her hand.

'Working out, much?' she teased. I was feeling better than I had in years thanks to Mum's swimming and the yard work, the home-cooked meals and Dad's relentless activities. Being home was like a fortnight at boot-camp.

We were the only boat at the fishing grounds. The sun gently warm in the clear autumn sky. Shelley climbed up onto the bow, waving her hand at me to get her a rod and rig it for her, and I obliged, remembering her favourite, knowing well she was capable of doing it herself.

As always, Dad was the first with a line in the water. He got River sorted next with short plastic Kmart rod rigged with a barbless rainbow squid-jig that she bobbed in the water and slapped around on the surface.

Hayden would have no part of the Kmart rod Dad offered him.

'I'm going to catch the biggest fish,' he said, trying to yank the rod I'd finished rigging for Shelley from my hands.

'This one is for your mum,' I said, yanking it back, surprised when I actually got away with it. Shelley shrugged, and cast in from the front of the boat.

'Which one do you want, champ?' I asked, and of course he pointed to Dad's grandfather of a rod. A huge wooden-handled beast I could barely cast myself.

'OK,' I said. 'But we'll share.'

Hayden loaded it up with sinkers of all shapes and weights. Guaranteed weed magnets. Then I attached a whiting trace from the set I'd made with Dad. I helped him cast, and let the weight of the rod rest in my palm.

We drifted.

Shelley said, 'When did you last talk to her?'

I leaned against the gunwale. 'Before I came up here.'

'Not since? Not even texting?'

'Or Facetime?' Mum asked.

I smirked. 'What's there to Facetime about, Mum?'

'Don't you still love her?' Shelley asked, in her typical straight-for-the-jugular style.

The butt of Hayden's rod quivered in my hand. 'You right, mate? You got something?'

Hayden reeled.

'Like this,' Dad said, leaving River at the stern and coming to teach Hayden how to be a man better than I ever could.

'Ben?' Shelley prompted.

'Yes,' I said, annoyed. 'Yes of course I still love her.'

'So fix it,' Mum said. 'Whatever's wrong between you two, sort it out.'

'It's not that simple.'

'It is,' Mum said. 'It is that simple.'

Dad nudged me. 'Give us some space, Ben,' he said, backing into the boat, struggling with the weight of the rod, the fish, and all of Hayden's sinkers.

I stepped towards Mum, shifting the weight of four adults to the one side of the vessel. The boat pitched. Mum gripped the gunwale. River squealed. Shelley's thighs screeched across the aluminium as she slid toward the bow railing.

'Jeeze, Ben,' she said with her ice-glare. She strained her neck to see past the console to the stern. 'You OK, honey?'

'River?' Mum called.

It was Dad who got to her first and settled her back onto the seat.

Alone with the rod, Hayden lurched, the full weight proving too much as the fish made a final fight near the surface. And simple as that, Hayden, with his rod, was hauled over the side.

I had every lifesaving and water safety certificate known to Queensland. Bronze star, bronze medallion, bronze cross. I knew you should only ever, *ever*, go in the water as a last resort for rescue. None of that mattered in that moment. I didn't think twice. I pulled off my shirt and in I went, like The Hoff in his prime, leaping from the gunwale in my Baywatch-red boardshorts. Cold blasted my skin as I plunged into the ocean. I pushed back to the surface and swam the few strokes over to Hayden. With the sound of my family carrying on in the background, I reached out for him.

'It got away,' he said, his face twisted with anguish.

'It's OK,' I said. 'I've got you.'

I pulled him toward me easily, buoyant in his clipped-up yellow vest. When I tried to get my arm around him, he slapped at me frantically.

'Get off. Get off. GET OFF.'

He kicked out, his feet connecting with my stomach. The air rushed out of me. I doubled over, my head sinking under. I sucked in water instead of air. When I found the surface, coughing, I saw the back of Hayden's damp little head, motoring away from me. Back to the safety of the boat, arms outstretched. And Mum, waiting at the side with her healing hands, ready to pull him in.

Everything and nothing

Joint accounts

I can hear them at the next table talking about money. I can't hear every word, but I know the script. I've practised it myself. According to the book, it's a conversation meant to be had in a fancy restaurant. So here I am, and so are they, it seems, in the only flash place in town. One with tiny tables that the staff have to pull out so you can squeeze in to your seat. Here, wine is only sold by the bottle and when purchased and poured it's removed from your table and stored in elevated stainless steel ice buckets that need to be moved every time someone wants to get up to go to the bathroom. Excuse me, excuse me. Sorry. I've been too scared to drink more than half a glass because I don't know what happens when I need a refill. The bottles have been moved so many times it's like a sideshow game of watch the ball at sixty dollars a try, and I can't remember which bucket is mine.

I smooth the white tablecloth under my palm, and wait for Will's attention. The light from his phone screen illuminates his chin like he's about to tell a ghost story. 'Don't stop,' he says, not looking up.

Before I can go on, the waiter arrives with the garlic bread. The woman beside me glances over. Garlic bread is delivered to their table, too. I tell the waiter we're sharing and there's a moment of confusion because he doesn't know if I mean with the next table. I gesture at Will. The dishes are set down and the woman looks away with an apologetic smile. It's impossible not to be joined in some way by our proximity. But we're also joined by our intentions and it's clear her set menu is going better than mine. When the waiter offers to pour more wine, we both say *please*.

I can smell my own sweat as I raise my glass. It was mistake to pair a synthetic dress with stress. I drink the wine down to match the level of Will's glass before he notices. Tonight was meant to be about sharing equally, after all.

Will clicks his phone off. The ghostly look doesn't leave his face. 'What were you saying about buckets?' He clocks our near-empty wine glasses and clicks for the waiter. I want to say, *I'm sorry, excuse me* and never come back. Slowly, slowly, I slip the pen and notepad back into my clutch purse. The little jotting pad was an afterthought. I didn't think the restaurant would appreciate me scribbling our Serviette Strategy on the back of their starched linen napkins.

'Never mind,' I say as more wine is poured.

'Don't do that. You were saying something. About joint accounts.' He walks his fingers across the table and digs them under my palm. 'The thing is …' A thin smile. 'It's just difficult to tie everything up like that. I need to be flexible for work.'

'For work?' I withdraw my hand, fold it in my lap.

'I'm serious about us.' *But.* He sits back. 'This is better for you, trust me.' He lets out a breathy laugh on the word trust, like I don't know the half of it. 'Joint accounts would just complicate things.'

'Things are already complicated,' I say, because he doesn't know the half of it.

At the next table, the couple have their phones out and are setting up their joint accounts. The screens show the orange promise of no fees. They'll be onto sorting out their superannuation before the mains arrive. I don't even know if Will has superannuation. Or if he owns his car. Or if I love him. Or if I want to keep the baby. He looks at the garlic bread going cold between us like he can't work out how it got there.

'I need to go to the bathroom,' I say, looking for a way out.

Will slides back his chair and from nowhere a team of waiters wordlessly arrive to begin the process of shifting everything to accommodate my exit.

'I'm sorry,' I say to Will as I squeeze past him. 'Excuse me.'

Mojo

'I need two grand for my mojo.' Beer slops out of Pam's pint as she nudges her way onto our table. I push a coaster over the slop, but Poppy goes one better with a little packet of tissues that she retrieves from her bag without ever taking her eyes off Pam.

'You're actually reading the book?' Poppy's asks, as she sops up the mess. Her hands are slender and well-moisturised, but tough-looking. There's grease under her manicure. She plops each of the soggy tissues into an empty beer glass and takes it to the counter. The men in the room, and there are plenty of them, watch her walk there and back on her long brown legs. She gets a lot of business with those legs.

Pam barks, 'Quit ya gawking,' at the blokes as she wrestles a stool over to our table. She sits on it so heavily the air escaping the cushion makes a sound like it's been punched in the guts. *Oopphf.* To me Pam says, 'You can have it when I'm done.'

Poppy agrees, 'It's life changing.'

I've actually read the book they're talking about. Years ago, before it got famous again. I've read lots of books. *Feel the Fear and Do It Anyway, The Power of Positive Thinking.* They were meant to help me so I could help Pam. Pam's not exactly open to change. Even in the thick of losing her boy, grief was as mundane to her as period pain, or long queues at the supermarket checkout, or electricity bills. And my grief turned quickly to resentment. Thanks mostly to the fifty grand of millennial debt my dead fiancé lumped me with. So, I put down the self-help books and picked up the finance books. We were still called Generation Y then. The Millennial thing came later.

Pam slurps on her beer. 'So, I need ideas. Poppy, how'd you get your mojo?'

Poppy puts the packet of tissues back in her purse. 'I don't have mojo,' she says. She twirls her five-dollar glass of house white by the stem. 'I've got cars.'

'What's the emergency?' I dare to ask. Pam's last emergency was her second son's funeral. Two sons, two funerals. I'd paid for both.

Pam looks at the door. 'I don't know yet.' She drinks her beer with great contemplation. The blast of air-con coming from the pokie room slips around my ankles. Poppy looks up at me like she's snuck into my thoughts. She gives me one of her calming long-lashed take-a-breath looks, her speciality anytime there's a risk Pam might mention Sean.

Poppy says, 'Have you been down to see the seal?'

We leave after the third round. The breeze is up and carries the smell of salt and possum piss from the overhanging trees and fish guts from the boat ramp. We cross quickly through town and down to the boat ramp. Pam slaps along in her worn-down thongs, tugging at the hem of her denim skirt, rushing to keep pace with Poppy's stride.

'I don't miss that smell,' Poppy says, scrunching her nose.

The seal is an annual novelty. A rarity in Queensland waters, especially this far north. For the past three years it's shown up for a few weeks each spring, chasing kids and dogs, stinking up the place and then vanishing before the council can erect any warning signs. I have a soft spot for the seal.

'Maybe we should go in the morning?' I suggest. 'After the high tide.'

'It could be gone in the morning.'

When we get to the beach, we're the only rubberneckers braving the low tide stench. The seal is up on the rocks. A heaving blob of mottled brown and grey, pink belly up, scratching its ear with a flipper.

'It looks different to last year,' Poppy says.

'It's the same one,' I say. I could evidence this claim with photos but I don't want to take out my phone. I'm a day behind on my payments. That's usually when the threats start coming in. The tide has sucked out, leaving a stretch of rippled wet sand. I wonder if the seal has had dinner. I scan the beach for approaching cars, worried about the potential for accidents.

'Worse than hitting a roo,' Poppy says, in my head again. 'Great for business.'

We watch in zoo-like fascination. The three of us standing in a line, mesmerised, until march flies flock to us. Pam swats my shoulder blade. Misses. 'Sorry.'

The seal gives a wide-mouthed grunt and blusters fishy breath our way. The smell is worse when it rolls over, as though activating a scratch and sniff panel.

Pam says, 'We could sell Sean's truck.'

'My truck,' I say, realising she's back on about her mojo.

Poppy rescues, 'You wouldn't get more than five-hundred for the parts.'

'That's a start.'

'Then what will Leah drive?'

'Sean would want what's best for me. He'd want me to have mojo,' Pam says and I can't stop myself thinking Sean has been dead five years now. I don't think what Sean wants is all that relevant anymore.

'Fine,' I say. I dig in my pocket for the key. It takes yonks to wind it off the metal loop. I toss the key to Pam. 'Go on, then. Chop it up.'

Income

Poppy wakes with the sun. Sitting up, she retrieves her blanket from the floor, trying to remember which of her dreams had made her fight it off. The polished concrete is cool underfoot as she goes to the sink to wash her face. The rod on the blinds clanks against the window frame. The wind has changed. Twisting the blinds open, Poppy squints as the sun blasts in. The bright morning illuminates her workshop. Out there, the Pacific glitters. She slides the windows open and the sea air is a refreshing change from the wafting stench from the seal.

Poppy mixes up a glass of cold water with the juice of half a lemon and drinks it down as she unlocks the sliding door and goes out to the verandah. Under the decking, the high tide laps at the pylons. Be careful about rust, her Redlands friends warned when she told them she wanted to buy the old VMR headquarters up north. Rust didn't scare her as much as being trapped forever in the shitty suburbs of her youth. So, she bought the book and planned to turn her tap on full.

Poppy was sceptical, at first. The author looked like a cross between Jamie Oliver and Lincoln Lewis. She liked Jamie Oliver and she once went to school with Lincoln Lewis but together there was something off-putting about the too clean, too friendly, too blond cover image. Her opinion changed as she got to know him through his printed advice. She liked his straight-talking attitude. His appetite for doing the work. He seemed, to her at least, a man of action. You want to double your income? Work twice as hard. You want money in the bank? Don't spend it. All of this made sense to Poppy who saved her way out of Capalaba and then out of Marcoola and on to Rainbow Beach within a year. For twelve months, Poppy worked Saturdays, without question. She did cashies on the side. She sold everything she could spare. The exception was her cars. Classic cars were her long-term investment. Her grow bucket. Talk about low-fee high return. She picked up shells from all over the county for as little as five hundred bucks and restored them to their original condition. Better than flipping houses. Poppy could turn a carcass into a fifty-grand beauty in a matter of months. The problem, though, was she often didn't want to let them go when she was done. She wouldn't go as far as to say cars had souls, but they sure did have history, and history was Poppy's Achilles heel.

Tying back her hair, Poppy takes a few deep breaths, then salutes the sun several times through. Variation A, then B. A few back bends. Child's pose. The breeze tickles along her long, curved spine as she stretches on the verandah. When she's stalled all she can, she gets changed, opens the roller door and stares down Sean's truck. Today, and she really has stalled as long as she can, Pam will get her mojo. She swings open the driver's-side door and pulls herself up with the handholds. The interior smells like Leah's green tea body spray. But there is evidence of Sean here, too. His Ray Bans are still on the dash. It's his keyring that Leah still used. Poppy slips the key into the ignition and starts the truck with a vibrating roar. Poor Leah. Pam really was doing her a favour by removing this heap of shit from her life. Poppy lets it run, listening for any warnings in the engine. The sound takes her back to the fights Sean and Leah used to have about this truck, and money. Mostly the truck, though, because Sean had thrown a dumb amount – a reckless amount – of cash at it. No wonder Pam thought it was worth something. In truth, goods and services had been exchanged so Leah could be haunted by a poorly rigged machine full of dodgy workmanship and stolen parts. The truck, like their relationship, was unroadworthy. That's why Leah had never sold it. Couldn't get a bean for it. Instead she'd sold her perfectly respectable and reliable second-hand Hilux ($6,250) and was left with this monster. God it was an embarrassment. Loading groceries in with Leah was the worst. Townies looked at Leah like she was some bogan's girlfriend. She was too. A bogan's fiancée to be exact. Or she was until Sean got himself killed and lumped Leah with his ridiculous debt.

Poppy rolls the truck into her workshop, then shuts off the motor and climbs down out of the cab. The night before she'd laid out her tools like a surgeon ready for work. Her gut had been troubling her all week. Not in a sick-tummy kind of way, but her gut. This is meant to be the fun part of her job but her insides were on high-alert. Poppy selects a newly charged battery off the rack and slots it into her Makita drill. It's just business. Why does she feel like it's Sean she's about to hack up? Besides, she's already given Leah two weeks to change her mind.

'Hello?'

A city bloke lurks by the door. Polo shirt tucked into jeans. A square chin. Not another one. Townies she meets at the pub are always wandering down this way once they get wind of where she lives.

'Can I help you?'

'A guy down the boat ramp told me you do towing?'

Poppy lowers the drill. 'Are you bogged?'

Walking towards him, Poppy takes a better look at the man in her doorway. He's average in every way. Height, build, hair colour. He has the kind of face Poppy wouldn't remember if she had to pick him out of a lineup. But for some reason she doesn't think she'd ever need to. He seems trustworthy.

'Not exactly.'

'High tide catch you?'

He turns and looks down towards the beach. The morning sun catches the side of his face. Average might have been a cruel assessment. Maybe he's one up from average.

'Have you rolled it?'

He swallows. 'Maybe you could come take a look?'

The side gate bangs closed and footsteps rattle up the fire stairs.

Poppy's stomach flutters. She steps closer to her tool bench. Sweeps her eyes over the offerings. Stanley knife. Crowbar. Mallet. 'Where did you say you're from?' she asks.

'North,' he says. Then adds, 'Inland.'

Seconds later Leah is at the sliding door. The front of her shirt is damp, her face flushed pink. The smell of bleach comes inside with her. 'Thank god,' Leah says, breathless. Her eyes look like they are ready to release tears. She wipes her face. Stands straighter. She's come straight from her cleaning job. A rescue mission. Poppy feels energy zap around the room.

When Leah doesn't say anything more, the bloke rubs his nose, folds his arms. 'Honestly,' he says, like he's making a confession. 'I didn't know you had seals here.'

Insurance

She doesn't let me pick her up. Maybe she thinks if a bloke can't handle an Isuzu on soft sand he's not to be trusted. Maybe I'm not. Or maybe she's too embarrassed to be seen in the rental truck I was stuck with. Some jacked-up ute with spotlights and roll-bars. Still had the last driver's sunnies on the dash. Really not my style. I'm guessing not her style, either.

The pub is on the main street. A few blocks back from the beach. The day is holding the light so I decide to walk and add myself to the queue on the phone to my insurer while I'm at it. My call is important to them. I'm currently in position twenty-two. I hang up. Meeting her has been the only bright part of my day. I'm hoping it's about to get brighter.

The heavy glass door at the pub promises two for one drinks on Tuesday and I can see from the crowd inside they deliver on their promise. I push on the door and go into the crowded chill. Everyone looks at me like they already know. Nudging my way through the crowd of bargain drinkers, I see I've already been added to the Rainbow Beach Towing wall of shame.

'Seal killer,' someone jeers.

It's a misplaced slur. I squeeze onto the bar and wait for the bartender to drift in front of me. 'I didn't even hit the seal,' I tell him. He shrugs and pours two pints, even though I've only ordered one.

'I don't want two.'

'The second one is free.' I don't argue with his logic.

Across the bar Poppy stands proudly at the pin-board, a pint of white wine in her hand. Her two drinks poured manageably into one. She has the crowd rapt. Thought it was a rock. Hahaha. I move to a table with my cumbersome beers and wait for Leah knowing she's going to be the one to recuse me.

She arrives to the table in a summery dress. Pale blue and fitted at the waist. She has followed Poppy's lead with the pint of white wine.

'Cute dress.'

'Thanks,' she says, and adds, as if on cue, 'It has pockets.'

We leave the pub after the first round and head to the surf club, prepared to pay the higher price for a bit of peace. Below, low tide has turned the beach into a highway. The traffic queueing at the off-ramp. Streams of campers flowing in and out of the shower blocks. The seal stands guard from the safety of his rock, barking at the line of cars.

'Must have given you the fright of your life,' Leah says.

'I was not expecting a seal, or traction control.'

'It doesn't take much to flip out there.'

'I bet you've been driving on the beach since before you could walk?'

'Nah,' she snorts. 'I'm not from here.'

'Seems no-one is.'

My phone buzzes, lighting up my pocket. 'Sorry,' I say. I can't help but check the message before holding in the button to turn my phone off. All the way off. Like, off off.

'Ex-girlfriend?' Leah jokes.

'Worse. The bank.'

That gets a good laugh out of her. I sit back in my chair and take in the view.

Debt

'She's just obsessed with it,' I say. 'Like a pusher. I can't have a conversation without her bringing it up, promising how it will change my life. Have you read it?'

'I've read it, yeah.' Will dusts the chicken salt off his fingers. 'Mia was as bad as Poppy. I took her out to dinner to propose, really fancy place. And she was just would not shut up about joint accounts. It's like the combination of wine and garlic bread triggered her.'

I try to picture Sean proposing in a restaurant and can't. He was more the KFC in the back of the ute at the lookout kind of guy. Instead he'd proposed to me at our year twelve formal. That was the norm for high school sweethearts, right? He'd hidden the ring in the box for the corsage, but Pam was late picking up the flowers. And the ugly white limo was already there and I told him not to worry about the corsage, to just hurry up. Maybe it was the bite of guilt that made me say yes, later, when Pam arrived and stood by looking on expectantly. We'd buried Sean's brother two months earlier. None of us were thinking straight.

'What happened?' I ask Will because he seems familiar to me, like we've both made the same lucky escape.

Will taps the table, as though working through the he-said she-said of the night all over again. 'She did a runner.'

'I'm sorry.'

'Don't say that.' He gestures at the diamond ring on my right hand. 'What about your guy?'

'Also did a runner,' I laugh. I slip the ring off and push it to the middle of the table. 'It's probably stolen.'

'Why do you keep wearing it?'

'Nostalgia. For his mum, maybe. I don't know.'

When he gets up to go to the bathroom, he leaves his phone on the table. It's in one of those leather wallet-cases that also holds cash and cards. I can't help myself. I flip it open. Slide his hotel keycard out to check where he's staying. Pinch a bit of cash. The single key for Sean's truck is tucked inside one of the card slots and I slip it out and into the pocket of my dress with the money. I place the phone back exactly where he'd left it.

When he gets back to the table, he seems surprised I'm still there. Mia has given him a complex.

'I can sell it for you,' he says of Sean's ring. 'I had to get rid of one myself, recently.'

'You probably had all the right paperwork.'

Will raises his drink and looks at me over the rim of his glass. 'Not necessarily,' he says. 'There are plenty of ways to fill up buckets.'

'I already work eighty hours a week,' I say.

He leans in. 'Don't you get tired of doing the right thing all the time?'

'I should probably check on Poppy,' I say, standing.

'Yeah, OK,' he sighs, like he was expecting this all along. He scoops the ring off the table and thrusts it at me. 'Don't forget this. You're obviously not over him.'

Out on the street, the night sky waits for the stars to come out. I join the queue at the ice cream shop and order passionfruit to get the taste of booze out of my mouth. I put Sean's ring in my pocket with the key for the truck. I'll swipe the ute from Will's hotel carpark overnight. By morning, it will be parts in Poppy's workshop. My own plastic surgery. My own way to get my mojo back. I don't go to check on Poppy. Instead I head down to the beach to sit with the seal while I finish my gelato.

The rocks are still warm from the daylight. I watch the heave of the seal's belly while it sleeps.

Author's Note The advice followed by the characters in this story is inspired by Scott Pape's *The Barefoot Investor* (Wiley, 2017)

The Beachcombers

Flotsam /ˈflɒtsəm/ [ˈflotsuhm]

noun

such part of the wreckage of a ship or its cargo as is found floating on the water or washed up by the sea.

The back of his throat burns. Eddie rolls onto his side and his head reels catching up with him. One eye is caked shut with salt. The other is closed desperately tight against the sun. He pushes himself up onto one elbow, then the other. On hands and knees, he tries to spit but his mouth is dry. Sand crunches between his back teeth. His lungs are raw. His chest rattles.

On the sand he rests on his knees. With his eyes still painfully closed, he touches each tender part of his body. His shoulder, his neck. Chest, abdomen, thighs. With his waterlogged fingertips he catalogues his damage. There are no broken bones. No cuts that won't heal. He has escaped from the sea, from tragedy. Eddie laughs. His lungs rasping. He is soaked and spent but he is alive.

Planting both fists hard into the ground, he pushes himself up. As he staggers upright, his ears prick at the shuffle and squeak of footsteps through hot sand.

'Who's there?' he says, his eyes still refusing to open.

A woman's voice coils into him like wood smoke. He rubs his palms against the crunch of salt-dried skin. Licks his fingertips and works the sand from his eyes. Blinking, light flaring, slowly, she comes into focus. Her skin is rubbed brown with freckles.

'Stop looking at me like that. I didn't rescue you.' She walks a slow circle around him. 'Where's your shirt?'

Her own clothes seem to have travelled with her from an age ago.

Eddie asks her, 'How did I get here?'

'You swam, I guess.'

Wading through his hangover, Eddie searches for the lost part of last night. They had taken the boat out after the wake. And sometime in the night, he had gone into the water.

'Get tipped in the storm?' she suggests.

He remembers storm clouds. Wind bullets. Squalls. He remembers drinking until the sky blurred. Did the boat go down? Or did he?

'Went overboard?'

'I don't know.'

She quits her pacing and comes to look him over. Nose to nose, she seems ageless. Her skin is smooth, unlined, coloured by the weather like an autumn leaf.

'Well, what's your plan, then?'

'My plan?'

She nods. 'You staying? You going? What?'

His focus breaks a boundary. He's been through hell and wound up here. On a beach that stretches so far it fades into the horizon. But where is here, exactly?

'Do you have a phone?' he asks.

'Want to call the friends who left you behind?'

Eddie doesn't bite. 'I was thinking of a taxi.'

Her laugh is sharp and cruel.

'What's so funny?'

'No taxis.'

'No?' Scepticism tugs at his words.

'No phones either.'

'None?'

'You're on an island,' she says.

Eddie's pulse is in his ears. Blood thumps inside his skull. The horizon mocks with its glimmering stretch of unforgiving blue.

'Which one?' he asks.

Defiantly, she says, 'Mine.'

Jean Sewell's home is built high on a rocky headland that marks the most eastern point of the coastline. The location, Jean admits, is precarious but necessary. Each day, she scrabbles down over rock and shale to the beach, and when the day is done, she lunges up again. There has been some effort, Eddie notes, to make a set of stairs, a safer pathway up the headland. A series of rock retaining walls mark an attempted goat track, but the soil that's gathered in these concrete pockets has sprouted cobbler's pegs and prickly pear, transforming the landings into defensive garden beds. So, over the rocks they go. Jean's heels dry and cracked like creek beds, and Eddie's sensitive town-toes following.

At the summit sits the house. A simple three-room cottage constructed on a slab. Some mixture of magic and engineering holds the house in place. The thick slab balances on as much air as rock. As Eddie steps onto the patio he braces himself for a landslide. But the foundations hold, for now. From the beach, the house looked pristine, but up close, here on the headland, the window shutters are mildewed and the front door hangs on bent hinges. The house could be as old as Jean. Or older.

As Jean shows Eddie through the rooms, he sees she has made a substantial life here at the edge of the sea. The house isn't some shambled makeshift shelter. There are light bulbs and pipes, a maze of waterworks and wiring. Jean, or someone, has built this home for her.

Following her through to the only bedroom, a cot made-up with bedclothes tucked military-tight, Eddie asks 'What are you doing living out here?'

'I'm keeping watch.'

'For what?'

'Ships.'

'Illegal ships?'

'Just ships. Boats. Skiffs. Liners. Tugs. Doesn't matter who's on them. Can't tell from here anyway.'

Eddie chews it over. Wonders if too much salt air has rusted some of Jean's circuits. He says, 'You know the war ended fifteen years ago?'

The way she looks at him makes him think that it's been her dutiful gaze that has kept the country safe all this time. 'Exactly,' she says.

With a last flourish of her hand, Jean displays the final room with pride. They have returned to the sitting room and kitchen, where a long table faces the windows, the surface spread with maps and charts. Hanging from a stern-backed wooden chair is a pair of binoculars, and in the corner of the room, a telescope stands with the lens trained on the Pacific. The kitchen occupies the same space with a deep washbasin and high cupboards, some missing their doors. With clean floors and minimal furniture, the house would be neat, except each shelf in each room is filled to the brim with found objects.

Eddie drifts back through the sitting room, naming things in his head. Glass bottles, shells, driftwood, scraps of worn plastic, barnacled buoys. And other things too, things more mysterious. A Barbie head with the ponytail still intact. A single green and gold Australia Day thong. A length of galvanised chain. Fishing reels. A video tape. Eddie inspects the objects with his arms folded over his chest. His pants, now dry, chafe his inner thighs.

As Jean ferrets about in the bedroom, Eddie calls, 'What is all this stuff?'

There must be a decade of junk stored in this room alone. The word *beachcomber* comes to mind.

'What do you think it is?' Jean says when she returns to the doorway.

Shit. Eddie wants to say. Her house is full of shit. He thinks of his wife's determined mountain of throw-pillows on the bed she'd left behind and wonders why Jean's collection of decorations seem less garish.

Jean waits him out. Eventually she says, 'You don't know much about the ocean, do you?'

Eddie has long believed to know a little bit, almost enough, about everything.

Jean says, 'It's flotsam and jetsam.'

She picks up an off-white ping-pong ball and balances it in the palm of her hand.

'Flotsam,' she says. 'Things that float.'

She tosses the ball to Eddie who catches it easily from the air. He puts it back on the shelf and watchesA as Jean inspects the rest of her collection. She settles on a silver teaspoon, holds it up to him. The curve of the metal catches the light and reflects it on the wall.

'Jetsam,' she says. 'Things that sink.'

For someone so lean, Eddie notices now, Jean's clothes seem to bulge on her. She looks over the teaspoon for a moment then lays it back on the shelf. She begins to produce other items from her pockets. A knot of rope. A wooden clothes peg. A strawberry Chapstick. If there is any order to where she places things on the shelves, Eddie can't work it out. Jean ignores him as she finishes unpacking her treasures. Had she brought Eddie here to sit him on the shelf among all her other gatherings? For he too had gone overboard, the ocean had turned him over, tumbled him, and spat him out here on Jean's island. He was flotsam or jetsam. Just which, he couldn't yet tell.

With her pockets empty, Jean resumes her natural shape. She is strong boned, lined with muscle and sinew. Her ribs show between her breasts.

She goes back into the hall and comes back with a bundle of grey and navy clothes.

'You can put these on,' Jean says, handing them to Eddie. 'There's fresh water and soap in the washtub out back.'

Eddie accepts the clothes. Heavy work-trousers and a plain t-shirt. The fabric is starched and pressed. They have not been pulled from the ocean.

Eddie says, 'Does this happen often?'

'Does what?'

'Strangers washing up on your doorstep?'

Jean narrows her eyes at him. 'Are you a stranger now?'

Treading carefully, Eddie says, 'I don't have to be.'

'Good,' Jean puts her hands on her hips. 'Because I'm not running some drop-in centre if that's what you think. If you want to stay, you'll have to work. But for now, get cleaned up. I'll make tea. Then we can talk about what we're going to do with you.'

What was she going to do with him? He didn't know himself. For the fifteen short years he had been a husband, ten of those had been spent working for his wife's aunt as her carer and nurse. Despite her ailments, Nikki's aunt was a stalwart old chook and Eddie was genuinely fond of her. She'd given him a month off from his duties following Nikki's passing. 'For rest and recovery,' she'd said with a wink. 'For *your* well-being.'

Eddie didn't know how she'd kept it together as the orderly from her new care-facility wheeled her away from him. His wife had only been gone for a week and he still felt like he could break at any moment.

After dinner, Jean offers Eddie two options. He can work at getting home, or he can work for her. She is getting on, after all, and good help on her island is hard to find. The house, she noted, needed a few touch-ups and Jean was about to start her annual batch of preserves so she could have fruit through the winter.

Or, he could make a bonfire, Jean suggested.

He could spell out an SOS with branches from the casuarina.

She had an old skiff that he could patch, row himself to the mainland.

'How far is it?' Eddie asked.

Jean waved her hand toward the ocean. 'Depends on which current you aim for.'

She suggested Eddie sleep on his options. No phone. No radio.

Eddie thinks about it through the night. He thinks about it as they rise for breakfast. And the more Eddie thinks about ways to escape, the more he sees that life here, with Jean, at least for a little while, might be just what he needs. With Nikki's aunt in care, without his work, without his wife, Eddie is in no rush to get back to the real world that has turned on him so viciously. Perhaps Jean Sewell is on to something out here, adrift in the Pacific. She doesn't seem displaced by her isolation.

'I'm not isolated,' Jean scoffs over breakfast. 'This island has everything you need, if you know where to look.'

What does Jean need a radio for? A telephone?

'What about your work?' Eddie asks as he tidies away the breakfast plates.

'You're the one who said the war was over.'

'But what if you need to report something?'

'If there's something to report, I report it.'

Eddie watches her. There is no flicker of doubt. No waver in voice, no diversion of eyes.

'Does someone come to check on you? Bring supplies?'

'Do I look like I need to be checked in on?' Jean scrapes her chair back across the slats and stands up. 'I said you could do what you want. And you can. But I don't have time to sit around talking about what might or might not happen.'

She snatches the plates and tosses them into the sink. Cold cloudy water slops onto the floor.

Eddie wipes his hands on the back of his pants. He says, 'Show me what needs fixing.'

As Eddie works, he tries to quiet the questions that bombard him about Jean and her island. She's not telling him everything. But maybe, for once, it's better not knowing. Jean has rattled him. In a good way. He's second-guessing himself after thinking for too long that he knew everything there was to know about, *well*, everything.

Before Jean, his life was so safely contained in his work and his home. A life built between two women he lived for. Nikki and her scaly old aunt. Every hiss and wheeze he could manage. Every ache and pain he knew what to administer, and how. His work, his home, his life was medicated.

Not here. Here, the work is a very different thing. Here, his work is fixing the roof. As Eddie climbs onto the roof to rivet the aluminium, he knows he is a bit out of his depth. And the work is slow going. His knees don't like the angle he's asking them to hold. His hands, so used to caring for elderly, paper-thin skin seem too soft for the island. Too soft for Jean who is calloused and thick-soled and weather-proof.

From his rooftop vantage, he watches Jean way below on the beach collecting eugarie from the waterline. She wades out to her ankles and wriggles her hips, her feet churning up the sand. Then she bends and drags her hands through the slurry, flicking her bounty into the bucket. More twisting. More scooping. He imagines the bucket brimming with shellfish. The pipi birds join her parade. She's at home here. She's at peace.

Beyond Jean, the ocean glitters blue all the way to the horizon. He squints into the distance, over the breakers out where the curve of the earth joins the sky in a haze. No boats today. Not a single mast or puff of steam on the whole horizon.

A light southerly is blowing across the island, cooling the back of his neck. And every now and then, Eddie's ears clip the sounds of his old life. A car grinding through the gears, a beat of music. Eddie works on, refusing to be haunted.

At dusk, Jean leads Eddie expertly down the headland, a bottle of beer in one hand and Eddie's fingers gripped in the other. She's put on a flowing smock with the front pockets stuffed with an assortment of things. Her toes curl over the rock, gripping with surety. Eddie continues to stumble, the balls of his feet hot and raw.

On the beach, Jean digs out a hole with a dessert spoon, working swiftly, but without hurry. She piles up the sand pushing it and patting it with the deftness of a ceramic artist. When she is finished, the hole is bucket-sized and slowly, it fills with seeping water.

'For you,' she says. 'For your feet.'

Eddie realises she has made a foot-bath with a steady back rest.

'Spared no expense,' he jibes. 'Is there anything you can't do?'

'You want it or not?'

Eddie swallows his smile. Settles into the seat. Instantly, his feet are soothed by the cooling salt-water. He digs his toes into the wet sand. Relaxing into the sensation.

'You sit tight,' she says. 'I'll build a fire.'

Eddie obliges, knowing better than to leave the spot she's made for him and insult her with offers of help. Instead he watches the sky sharpen in the fading light. The water darkening to indigo. The sun flaring orange.

Jean drags bark and wood and kindling from the scrub and makes a fire-pit. By the time the sun slips below the island, a blaze is roaring and Eddie can't remember the last time he felt so relaxed.

Jean settles on the sand beside him, half her face illuminated, the other half in shadow. Her profile is striking. The sweep of nose and cheek bones, the strength in her shoulders and chest.

'You're beautiful,' he says.

Her smile is careful. Ignoring him, she says, 'You'll have to keep the heat up if you want it to burn through the night. But don't smother it. Tomorrow, try for leaves and bark if you want a lot of smoke for the daylight. The tides from the full moon are starting to settle so you shouldn't have trouble here, above the waterline.'

'You didn't have to do this.'

'You think you want to stay forever. You don't.'

Eddie stands up and steps out of the hole she's dug him. His wet feet glisten pale and waterlogged. He rounds her and sits closer to the fire, stretching his legs out in front of him so the flames warm the soles of his feet.

'I don't like to think about forever.'

'Don't you have a lady back home? Someone who is missing you?'

Pushing aside thoughts of Nikki, Eddie nods. 'I've got a lady. She's like you.'

'What, old?'

Eddie laughs.

'I'm not so old.'

'That's what she says.'

Jean shrugs it off. Turns to him. 'What about the real one?'

'Nikki,' Eddie says. Beautiful, tragic, erased Nikki. He is surprised by how easily he can say her name.

'Nikki,' Jean repeats. 'Sounds like a beauty.'

'She was.' He wants to put his arms around her. He says, 'She was an artist, a sculptor.'

'That's noble.'

'Is it?'

He takes Jean's hand in his and unfurls her fingers one by one. He runs his finger across her palm, tracing her thick lifeline.

He says, 'Her hand was crushed. There was an accident when she was younger. Her parents died.'

He closes three of her fingers over one of his own. 'She lost these. But she lived.'

Jean shakes her hand free. 'Of course. You rescued her.'

'No,' Eddie says. He shakes his own hands out, drives them into the sand. 'I didn't save her.'

Jean picks up a stick and pokes at the coals. She says, 'You must make a lot of money, doing what you do.'

'Nursing?'

Jean shrugs. She says, 'I just can't imagine her being too productive –making art with only one hand.'

The barbs bite in exactly where she's aimed.

Eddie takes the stick from her. 'I didn't say she was perfect.'

'You didn't have to.'

The house is empty when Eddie wakes. He feels the absence of Jean before he confirms it by pacing through the rooms. He checks anyway, pushing on the door to her bedroom and leaning in. The bed is made up with perfect corners. The shelves above cluttered by trinkets and driftwood. In the kitchen he checks the clock and wonders if he has woken with her. For an hour or so he lay dead-still in his swag, tucked behind the table in the sitting room. He hadn't heard Jean leave. That didn't mean anything.

He remembers this connection with Nikki's aunt, becoming attune to her sleep patterns and her needs. He would wake at 2:30 for a glass of warm milk and again at 5:45 to help her to the washroom. With Nikki, he never found the link. He'd lie awake beside her wondering how she could sleep so easily on some nights, snoring softly into the side of his neck, while other nights she roamed and raged and didn't get a wink. She's always been like that – living in fits and starts. Always.

Lately, Eddie's been having doubts about her, about her passing, about their life together. Bitter creepy-crawly ideas have begun seeping in. Tiny barbed truths sneaking up and jabbing him in the sternum. How well-matched were they? How much did she really love him? Why didn't they ever have children of their own? Eddie had lost so much time thinking her damage was only to her hand. Was that a mistake of his trade? Was he so concerned with physical well-being that he'd neglected the true signs of Nikki's deterioration?

Her aunt said it best. 'If she's going, Eddie, she's already gone.'

And she was gone. She'd been gone for years.

Eddie puts the kettle on the boil and goes out with Jean's binoculars onto the patio. The day is overcast, the glare almost blinding. He scans the beach below and sees the fire has snubbed out. There is no sign of Jean. Not even footprints along the sandy shore.

He steps down from the slab onto the rock and rounds the back of the house. He takes a piss on Jean's Eureka lemon tree. Then wanders up a little further into the scrub. The bush at the top of the headland is thick with weed and vines. Lantana. Lawyer Vine. Even the grass rasps with stinging hairs. Eddie stands clear but peers in. What's through there, he wonders. He's only seen the sandy stretch of coast. Surely the island is more than this patch of beach, and one rocky headland.

The bush is too dense to fathom how far back it reaches. To get through, he'd want a machete. He'd want shoes. It must go somewhere. Eddie strains until his vision blurs. On the wind, he hears insects and birdcalls, he hears the creak and moan of boughs. He hears the chime of a telephone. Eddie stands abruptly, loses the thread of the sound. No amount of straining can pick it up again. Instead the whistling kettle calls to him. A pitch so high it rings between his ears and surges down his spine.

Eddie works on, the days the same, Jean the same, the house changing. Then, overnight, the beach changes too. The sea carves out a lagoon in close to the headland. The sand swept out and down the beach, forms a protective bank that holds back the swell and traps baitfish and whiting in the clear blue shallows on the afternoon low tide. Gulls and gannets bomb the shore, churning the surface with every catch and miss.

With the light fading and the sandflies biting, Eddie follows Jean down to fish for their dinner.

'We have to make the most of it before things change again,' Jean says.

Eddie is better with the cast-net than her. He holds it across his chest instead of over the shoulder. His throw is wide and strong. But even in the confines of the lagoon the tiny fish are too swift for him. As he gathers the net, pulling it closed, the fish slip and vanish between the holes.

'Makes you admire the birds,' Eddie says as he abandons the net and begins rigging up a line instead.

'I thought you said you didn't know much about the ocean?'

'I didn't say that.' Eddie puts the knot to his mouth, licking the line before pulling it tight between his teeth. 'You did.'

'Who taught you to fish?'

'Nikki,' he says. 'Before she was an artist, she used to work on boats. I'd buy prawns from her at Christmas. It's how we met. You thought I met her at the hospital.'

'I didn't say that.'

'But you assumed I only knew her *after*.'

Eddie tests the knot between his teeth and fingers. Threads salted eugarie onto the hook.

Jean is not listening to him. She has waded out and stands knee-deep in the lagoon, casting out onto the bank. He casts downstream then wades out to her. Around them, the baitfish swirl the ocean in a slick of black.

When he's finished with the roofing, Eddie turns his attention to the front door. He imagines gusts like fists battering Jean's house. Today, though, there is no wind. The clouds gather and hang low in the sky, trapping the salt air in thick humidity. Wrestling to hold the heavy door makes him sticky. He sheds his shirt, the buttoned cuff catching his wrist. He tugs against it, pulling his arm free. The relief triggers a memory. He remembers plunging into the sea, over the stern. He remembers the surge and foam of the water. How black it was. How turbulent.

And he remembers something else. Something coming at him from below as he wrestled from his funeral suit jacket. A sleek shape, fingertips grazing his skin, grabbing at him. Familiar hands. Billowing black hair. Someone, he's sure, had been trying to pull him under.

Eddie pushes into his memory, probes at the parts that have been closed away from him. The boat didn't sink. He knows, now. He remembers. There was a storm. There was music. There was too much to drink. Lightning. Chaos. But if the boat didn't sink, how did he end up in the water. Below the surface. Had he fallen overboard? Or had he jumped?

Eddie fishes a stubby Phillip's Head from his pocket and begins working free the rusting screws from the hinges. As he removes them one by one, each that comes free, he drops into the pocket of his pants. The screws rattle against other things he's stored in his pockets. Perhaps this is how it starts. Now, just like Jean, he's collecting things to carry, things to keep.

By mid-afternoon Jean has not returned. Eddie wonders about her absence. He's already grown accustomed to her and thinks that she should she have left a note. He's not worried for her well-being. It's him. He's missing her. Already, incorrectly, without invitation, he's begun to think of Jean as his companion. As a team mate. He believes in their duality.

Eddie needs to remember that Jean is an island. She has existed long before him, survived and thrived, and she will go on existing when he departs. For now, he is a tenant. A guest in her home. Her home. Not his home. He needs to remember this distinction. He needs to mind his own business.

With his daily tasks complete, Eddie is idle. He imagines wearing the floorboards thin as he paces the short length of hallway. He goes into the sitting room and looks out the window. No boats again today. He thinks he should mark it down, note it somewhere. This is Jean's work. Not his. If he were at home, at his home, what would he be doing now?

He can't remember. Or, more correctly, he doesn't know. He has only lived a handful of days without Nikki. The loss of her sounds loud inside him. He still forgets that she is gone. Eddie pitches forward and braces himself against the windowsill. She's gone.

Outside, the daylight is fading. He wants to avoid the scene where Jean arrives home – from wherever she's been –and finds him lurking. Eddie's existence is not dependant on her. He can make his own way.

When he closes the door, he's impressed by the smooth swing of the hinges, the graze and click of the latch. He's repairing things. This is his work. To heal. He might need Jean to survive here, but Jean, it seems, needs him, too. Eddie tumbles this around his head as he makes his way down to the beach.

There is new certainty in his gait. His feet have hardened, his lips have chapped. His hands are dark with ash and stain. He feels more equipped, somehow, better suited to living. Not just here, but anywhere. Imagine lifting Nikki's aunt now from chair to bed. Imagine combing out her hair. Taking her through her physio circuit, grasping her tiny foot in his hands, now hard and certain, flexing her knee.

But when he thinks of his hands on Nikki's aunt, it's Jean he imagines. Jean's foot. Jean's freckled skin. He undresses her. He wants to unpack the pockets of her smock, slip it over her head. He wants to care for her.

At the fire, the coals are cold. An unmistakable splash of hard sand travels across the fire-pit, through the soft dry sand where water has sunk in. Eddie kicks at the ash. Swears in a voice he doesn't recognise. He has been doused.

Nikki always made her decisions in retrospect. If her stomach fell, she knew she'd made the wrong choice. If she felt relief, she'd selected right. The problem with her method, Eddie always thought, was that her decisions – especially the last – had a striking finality. No take-backs. No second chances.

With the fire out, Eddie feels a new clarity. He rushes to rebuild it. He charges into the scrub grabbing deadwood and branches from swamp trees, from the ground sticks and leaves. He scrapes the pit clear, covers the wet sand with dry, and constructs the pyre with dry leaves and kindling.

Eddie's pockets jangle as he works. He pats down his pants. He has filled them. As he pulls objects from his pockets, he looks in awe at the things he has gathered. Rusty screws from the front door, sure. But what else does he have? A nob of soap, a scrap of rag, a plastic whistle, the head of a tooth-brush, a bottle of rubbing alcohol, a candlewick, a small knife. He has gathered these things, these useless things, but carries no matches. No light.

As Eddie turns from the fire to make his way back across the beach and up the headland, a glint on the horizon catches his eye. He turns his shoulders square to the sea and scans the ocean.

There.

A small sailboat, masts bare, skims behind the breakers. It's a pleasure ship. Unused to big swells, large journeys. On board a young couple dressed in linen, with bare arms and sunglasses that reflect the light back to him, train their binoculars on him.

Eddie raises one arm. Waves.

They wave back.

He waves again.

They lower the binoculars and exchange words.

What does he look like to them, with his workpants and bare chest, his desperate attempt at a fire? With the binoculars back on him, Eddie wonders what would happen if he ran down to the shore, both arms flailing in a desperate signal for help.

Jetsam /ˈdʒtsəm/ [ˈjetsuhm]

noun

goods thrown overboard to lighten a vessel in distress, which sink or are washed ashore.

On Monday, Jean Sewell rides her bicycle across the island and into town. Autumn has turned up the volume on the lorikeets and they shriek like a rainbow equaliser across the sky. Jean presses her face into the air, fills her lungs and pedals hard to keep up with them.

As dirt becomes gravel, then crumbled bitumen, then white-lined blacktop, Jean slows to catch her breath. She sets her shoulders into a memorised hunch, pedals with a rhythm more suited to the town. Everything is fine. Normal. She has nothing to hide.

This side of the island is sleepy. Unlike her wild, ocean-shored coast, here on the bayside life takes a slower pace. The community is home to settled refugees she'd supposedly meant to be keeping out.

In town, she rests her bicycle outside Goran's Roadhouse. Gathers her fuel can from the basket on the back of her bike, rests it on the ground and fills it with the steady stream of petrol. She taps her foot as the numbers flick over in the bowser. She can't remember the last time she felt so damn complete.

When she's filled her standard four litres, she pumps an additional five-hundred mil for good measure. Having a guest is doing no favours for her generator. A small price for the good he's doing.

Running the rest of her shopping list through her head, she makes her way into the roadhouse through the mesh and plastic fly-strips that hang from the doorway.

Behind the counter, Goran holds his arms out to welcome her.

'Jeanie,' he beams. 'Turned back any boats lately, my girl?'

'Quiet as ever,' Jean says as she gathers her provisions.

'Not even any subs?'

'Not that I've seen.'

This is the joke between them. Goran himself, like many others, arrived to the island by boat. He came from Serbia via Greece and Indonesia under Jean's watch. Jean would consider him her closest friend.

Goran chats to Jean about the nearing whale-watching season. Asks if she heard about the bloke who went overboard off a yacht last week. As Jean fills her arms with bundles of stock, she catches the gossip Goran hurls into the aisles. The store prides itself on being a true one-stop shop, and lucky for Jean, it is. For years Jean has relied on Goran's Roadhouse for her pantry staples, for her hardware and her fuel. She hasn't set foot on the mainland since before the war. Before her husband died.

As Jean finalises her purchases, Goran says, 'Suicide they reckon. Paper said he'd been having a rough trot. Lost his wife and topped himself. How'd that roof of yours hold up in the storm?'

'It's fine,' she says with a shrug. Everything is normal.

'I can send Miljan around to look at it?'

'No need,' Jean says, 'I've handled it.'

Though Jean's provisions are minimal the repacking of things takes time. After leaving the store, she finds a spot in the shade near the football fields and sets about deconstructing her purchases. On this trip, everything she has chosen must look like it has come from the sea or from the earth. She doesn't think of this as a deception, instead, she considers it protection. For Eddie. For herself. For their life together.

So, she pours the coconut milk from the tetra pack into a recycled plastic bottle, she tips the passionfruit from their plastic into her string bag. Everything must look weather-worn, found, scavenged. This is no small task. It consumes her day.

With her groceries in check, Jean snaps a branch from a bottlebrush and ties one end of her new spool of fishing line to the branch. She clips the rest of the reel to her bike-basket, tests the run of it with a good yank. Satisfied, Jean loads the rest of her things into the basket.

As she rides back across the island, she lets the line run off the spool, dragging the branch so the fishing line wears and tangles, catching leaves and debris. A kilometre from home, she pulls up on the gravel and begins the slow process of reeling it back in again. When she is done, the bundle of line looks washed up, like she's happened upon it by the creek.

Not for the first time, she wonders what Eddie might be doing in her absence.

At the base of the headland Jean stares up the rockface to her house. The climb has never seemed so steep, so daunting. In a few days she's become reliant on Eddie's youth. On the broadness of his shoulders, the sureness of hands, his vitality. Weighted with her shopping, with the jerry-can, her smock, Jean begins the slow climb up.

She needs to get serious about her future here, she thinks as she climbs. Her knees will go eventually. Her joints will cease. She's not as young as she once was. Not nearly as nimble. When the weather clears, when the days get longer and hotter, she'll ask Eddie to have another shot at building a staircase. She should prepare for the future now, before it's upon her. Before it's too late.

Jean's breath labours. The string bag cuts into her shoulders. The jerry-can slops fuel out the perished rubber seal. Before Eddie, she hadn't noticed how decrepit things had become. Everywhere she looks, things need work. The spokes of her bicycle have busted, her fingernails are split and cracked, the kitchen cabinets are going, so is her eyesight, and her hair. She is diminished beside him. A tired old woman in a tired old house, living a tired old life.

When she makes it to the patio, she drops her groceries onto the slab and leans heavily against the verandah posts, vacuuming air into her lungs. The wind has changed, blowing in off the ocean. They weren't expecting another storm, but the sky tells a different story.

'Eddie!' she calls between breaths. Her voice echoes back at her, bouncing off the front of the house.

Using the verandah post to steady her, Jean hauls herself up the final step onto the patio. The front door greets her with a renewed veneer, square on bright hinges. She almost doesn't recognise it as her own.

Inside, she plonks the groceries on the small kitchen table. The cabinets have been repaired. Their doors lacquered and closed neatly. The house seems brighter, cleaner somehow.

'Eddie?'

Jean leaves the kitchen and crosses the hall to her sitting room. The desk is clear of papers. The windows pulled tight against the northerly. Outside, the clouds are gathering momentum. She reaches for her binoculars but they are not hanging from the chair. She turns her back on the horizon and looks around the room. Why has Eddie moved her things? Her maps. Her files. Her newspapers.

Where has he put her binoculars?

She looks again out the window, ignoring the sky and instead focusing on the great expanse of sea. The surface is grey and chopped. The glare almost blinding. She squints through the salt-smeared glass. Unsure of her eyesight anymore.

Unlatching the windows, Jean pushes them open against wind. The panes resists, rattling in their frames in protest. She shoves until they catch on the wind, opening wide, clanging back flat against the house.

In spite of the breeze, Jean drags the telescope to the window and trains it on the small patch of sea, beyond the fishing grounds, north toward where she saw what she thinks she saw. The mainland is a haze. Just a smudge on the horizon. So faint you'd never notice it unless you knew where to look.

After several passes, Jean spots the vessel she's been looking for. She takes this as a bittersweet victory. Her eyes have still got it. She knows a boat when she sees one. Even just a glint between swells. But what has she lost in exchange?

She focuses on the lettering down the side of the hull. This boat is familiar. She doesn't need to check her logs, wherever the hell he's moved them, to know the sailboat is owned by a young couple from the north. They visit annually, before the whale migration and travel with pods on their sail home. They're nice enough people, known locally for making a low-fi doco of their adventures at the start of the peacetime. This early in the season there should only be two crew aboard. Husband and wife.

A gust barrels in, rocking Jean on her heels. The telescope shifts and it takes her several more passes to find the sailboat again. There. Tacking back, she finds it. They would have come in close to the island, she's sure of it. This couple are typical creatures of habits. Same boat, same route, same day, every year.

Jean exhales, calculating the hours, the tide, the winds that would have brought them close to shore. She can't know Eddie would have seen them. But she can guess.

How many crew? Eye pressed against the telescope, she concentrates on keeping her gaze steady. How many on board?

On the beach, rain follows thunder as Jean races to the fire-pit. The pyre is stacked, but unlit. The wood and bark unmarred by the lick of flame. As the rain thickens, she traces Eddie's footprints, his to-and-fro around the fire-pit. Up to the scrub and back, dragging wood and branches that swish like snake-tails beside his footprints.

Around the fire the sand is dishevelled, marked with kicks and scuffs and mounds. From the chaos, though, Jean follows one clear path that leads hurriedly to the waterline. Toeprints in bold exclaim their intention.

Jean follows to the shore-break and looks out toward the sea. Has he gone? Has he left her?

If Jean were Nikki, she would throw herself into the sand and howl her heartache to the moon until Eddie returned to her. But Jean is not Nikki. Jean is a survivor. She begins to deconstruct the pyre and divides the wood into two piles. One for small wood she can carry back up the headland and use on the burner and a second stack to move off the beach, to higher ground for safe keeping. As she works, her smock catches on splinters, tugging and pulling. Her back aches with every heave. Her legs burn from the ride across the island. But Jean Sewell will not quit. She has lived without Eddie and she can go on without him. With every branch dragged from the pit, all Jean really wants to know is has this been a rescue from the island, or an escape from her?

With the wood cleared, Jean is making her way back to the headland when a wail like a storm-bird punctures the sky. Jean turns back to the beach. Something is rushing at her through the bushes. Jean drops the wood and backs toward the ocean, bundles her smock, preparing to run. Her muscles coil and tense. Ready to fight or take flight.

From the bush, Eddie lurches forward through the dark undergrowth. With binoculars slung across his chest, he looks like an explorer lost to the wilds. But Jean knows better. The bottom of his pants are shorn off and tied as makeshift booties around his feet. His shins are shredded and bleeding. His shirt is torn. The scrub, she knows, is unforgiving. Jean would take her chances with the sea over the island's inland any day.

He calls out to her in a voice choked with agony and rage. A bubbling of noises from some deep dark place within. He's gone wild. Gone too far into the depths of the island. Even though he's here, Jean wonders if he has already departed. And if so, has she become the outcast? The exiled?

Jean doesn't go to him. She stands her ground. The swell pulsing around her ankles, licking at her legs. This is her beach. Her island. Her home.

She waits.

Eddie clears the scrub, stumbling with fatigue and injury.

Slowly, Jean opens her arms to him. She holds them wide. Palms out. Not for an embrace, but for a redemption. She's been exposed, she knows. Her deception hasn't been taken lightly. She needs to turn herself out for him. Shed her skin. Let him decide for himself if what she is can be the thing he needs, the thing he trusts, or can trust again.

As Eddie comes forward, one agonised step at a time, Jean holds. She is nothing more or less than this. A lonely old woman at the base of her rock.

Maybe, to him, she is more than that.

She waits.

When he comes to stand before her, he won't meet her eyes. He is silent. Spent and flayed. She recognises the wounds from thorn and rock. Jean takes the weight of him. Her shoulder beneath his arm.

'It's a long way up,' she says.

She braces, but he doesn't take a step. Her own body aches from exertion. They stand together at the shore. Crutch and soldier. Only, Jean doesn't know which she is yet.

In the house, under the low electric light, Jean watches from the doorway as Eddie sheds the last shreds of his clothing and lays out – what's left of them – flat on the bed. Shirt, pants, scraps for shoes, creating the shape of a man raptured.

Naked, he begins the work on his body. With warm water clouded with antiseptic, he swabs it his cuts. With careful hands he plucks thorns and spines from his peeling skin. He takes his time with his grazes. Cleaning each rasp and tear with precision.

Jean marvels at how sturdy he is, how unflinching, how upright. This is what he's built for. Injury and wound. Tape and gauze. His body is no different to any other. As Jean looks on, he works as he would work with any other. Critical, severe, serious, moderate, minor. He knows how to heal.

When he is patched, he presses past her down the narrow hallway, barely an inch between them. She feels the heat of him as he passes. She watches as he selects a new set of clothes from the linen press. Her husband's heavy work trousers and a plain t-shirt. She has never known a body like his. As he dresses slowly, guiding the garments over his dressings, she knows she never will.

In the kitchen he draws a glass of water and sculls it down, leaning on the basin with one hand.

Jean says, 'I've got something harder, if you're interested?'

Eddie still doesn't look at her, keeps his eyes level at the window. She dares catch them in the reflection. Sees her damage bounce back at her.

'For the pain?' she suggests.

'OK,' he says.

They take the bottle onto the patio, sit with their legs dangling over the slab, the wind shaking the last drops of rain onto their faces. They go drink for drink, passing the bottle silently between them until the heat rises in Jean's chest.

'They think you're dead,' she says.

Eddie rests the bottle on his knee, clasps his thumb over the lip making it whistle. He adjusts his thumb so it becomes a low howl. A moan.

'Did you want to be?'

For the first time since the beach, he looks at her. 'What difference does it make?'

Jean keeps her eyes on his, takes the bottle from him and drinks a long slug. 'Plenty, I'd say.'

Eddie takes the bottle back. Matches her drink. As she watches, whisky glistens on her lips. When he lowers the bottle, he sets it on the slab and leans toward her.

With a slow, deliberate movement, he wipes his thumb heavily across her mouth. Watches the skin pull across her face. She's the most real person he's ever met. Why can't he believe in her?

'Why'd you run?' she says.

Eddie leans closer to her, trapping her between the verandah post and his battered chest.

'You lied to me.'

'I was helping you.'

'There are people here.'

Jean nods.

'A hundred metres down the beach there are access roads, tyre tracks.'

'That's right.'

Eddie nods. He says, 'It's not your island.'

'No,' Jean says. 'Not since the war.'

Eddie sits up. 'No phones?' he says, almost playfully.

'I didn't lie about that.'

Eddie brings the bottle back to his lap, picks absently at the label. 'Where did you go?'

Jean plays the day back in her head. Her own deceptions, her momentary insanity. It's almost laughable now. The lengths she was prepared to go to. More than that, she shouldn't have left him. She didn't think. She just didn't think. It dawns on her, finally, that maybe he wasn't trying to escape. Maybe, he was looking for her.

Jean puts her arm around him, pulls him close so her heart beats through her thin chest to his ear. She wants him to hear the hiss and thump, the tick and whirr of her beating heart. She hasn't left him. She is here. Alive.

'There was a boat,' he says.

'I know.'

When the repairs on Jean's home are complete, they begin work on Eddie's final project: the staircase. Jean traces out the safest path with a rusting can of silver spray paint, and though meandering, Eddie agrees it's the best route up the headland.

They can salvage some existing steps, and Jean leaves it to Eddie to pull up the prickly pear and clear the soil ready for laying over with gravel.

On hands and knees, Eddie works at each waypoint, pulling the weeds and cacti up and tossing them in his bucket. He rakes and turns the soil, looking for stray roots and seedlings. He's known the pear up close now, and it isn't something he wants to meet again with the bottom of his foot. As he pulls the plants up, he notices buds among the hair-like spines.

'They attract the bees,' Jean says dismissively when he asks about the flowers over lunch.

'Bees are good, Jean.'

'What's your point?'

'OK,' Eddie says flatly.

In the early hours of the morning, Eddie scrapes back the scrub near the Eureka lemon tree. He works the soil with a kitchen fork, clearing shale and pumice until he has a patch large as a dinner tray. He shovels in soil, building up the bed. Then he sets about replanting the budding prickly pear, careful to avoid the stinging bristles. He wants to give the chance of life. To bring bees to the lemon tree.

For the edging of the garden bed, Eddie mixes the last bucket of spare cement from the stair project. He lays a simple, low border around the garden, smoothing the edges. He is no match for wind or erosion, for storm or cyclone. But he can try.

With the border sculpted, he rests back on his heels and begins to empty his pockets. He takes out the rusting screws and bits of twig, the plastic clothes pegs and twisted bottle caps. These are the things he has gathered. These are the things he can leave behind. As he unpacks each object, he presses them into the drying cement, flotsam and jetsam alike, and tries to value them as useful or useless. It's no simple task. The boundaries for his definitions have changed. So has he.

He tells himself the garden isn't for Jean or for Nikki. It isn't for Nikki's aunt or for himself. Maybe it isn't even for the bees or the lemon tree. It's just a garden. He doesn't need to leave his mark on anything. Not yet.

Biography

Megan McGrath is an award-winning fiction writer from Minjerribah (North Stradbroke Island) in Queensland, Australia. She has written for *The New York Times*, *Meanjn*, *Griffith Review*, *Seizure* and *Tracks magazine*, among others.

Acknowledgments

Previously published stories as follows:

Tracks magazine (March 2015) 'Brother Bird', vol. 534, pp. 123

Tracks magazine (February 2016) 'The Cape', vol. 546, pp. 111

Seizure Journal (March 2013)

'The Breakers', [Online]

Available: www.seizureonline.com/content/the-breakers

Griffith Review (March 2010) 'The lunar coast', vol. 28, pp. 251-259

About This Series

Megan McGrath is runner-up in the 2019 Carmel Bird Digital Literary Award. The judge of the 2019 award was Australian author and academic, Moya Costello.

All Hands is published as part of the Spineless Wonders Smalls series of small format paperbacks released to celebrate our tenth year in publishing.

To find out about other books published in this series, go to www.shortaustralianstories.com.au

www.ingramcontent.com/pod-product-compliance
Lightning Source LLC
Chambersburg PA
CBHW030802190726
48285CB00003B/987